SNOWED IN KNOT

AMELIA SHAW

CONTENTS

ACKNOWLEDGMENTS

So grateful to the humans who made this book happen! Despite the popularity of AI in the world, I truly believe we need to support our artists and I'm doing my part by hiring as many people as I can to help me bring this book to life.
Thank you to:
My alpha reader Faedra Rose.
My editor, Carolyn from Write Right Edits.
My cover artist who designed the eBook cover, the paperback and all of the special edition pretties- Lori Grundy from Book Cover Design.
My character art artist Gombar Sanya.
My formatter Megan from Emcat Designs.

PROLOGUE

TILLY

The night before I turned eighteen, I fell asleep in my tiny bed with a twisting ache in my stomach. All too aware of what my future held as an omega in this town, I knew there was nothing that was going to change that for me.

My mother woke me early, with a whisper and a kiss to my forehead. "Baby, wake up."

I groaned and forced my heavy eyelids open. I'd been mid-dream and huddled under my thin blanket, barely warm enough, but still… it was too cold to get up and way too dark. "Mama? What's the time?" I asked, confused.

"Time to go," she said softly and pulled back the covers, causing the freezing morning air to steal across my body and rob me of the little heat I had garnered in slumber.

"But, Mama, it's too cold," I complained, only to have her pull me up into a seated position.

"You need to go, Tilly," she urged. "Go and never turn back."

"Huh?" I blinked my eyes to clear them and stood at her command, still running on autopilot.

She slid something around me that was thick, warm and very welcome. It was her coat—the only one she possessed. She encouraged me to slide my arms inside, then she pressed the handles of a tote bag into my hand.

I blinked groggily at her, still not with it. Was I still asleep? Was this all a random dream? None of what was going on made any sense.

What's going on here?

"Go? What do you mean, Mama?" I questioned. "Why? I don't understand."

She cupped my face with reverence and love that she'd rarely allowed herself to show me. "Because you deserve *so* much more than this life. Take your heat suppressors and don't settle for anything less than a true scent match, okay?"

"But…"

No, this isn't right.

I'd been told suppressors would mess with my heat cycles and my true purpose. Why would she be encouraging to take them?

She grabbed both of my hands and whispered fiercely, "Promise me you'll do as I say. I got you a three-months supply. They're already packed in the bag."

Hot tears welled in my eyes and slid down my cheeks, the last I would shed for years to come. "I promise," I answered, the words spilling from my lips despite the turmoil in my heart.

"Good girl. Now, pull your shoes on, and let's go. There's some cash in the pockets of the coat, but you'll have to get a job quickly because it will run out fast," she warned.

I didn't bother to ask where she got the money. My three Alpha fathers and three Alpha brothers made sure our mother never had a dime. That was a small part of the way they kept her beholden to them. She had no choice. With that bleak thought in mind, I pulled on my most comfortable running shoes, zipped up my mother's coat, and threw my phone and charger into the tote bag. I'd have to change the number for safety, but luckily the phone was an older model, and I very much doubted that it had the tech to be tracked.

We crept through the house together like frightened mice. The old wall clock ticked loudly in the silence, letting me know it was just after 4am.

Fuck. It's going to be freezing outside!

As Mama opened the back door, the rush of cold air that stole into my lungs made me gasp, and doubts crept in. "Are you sure I can't just..."

Go back inside. Back to my bed and the life that has already been planned for me?

"No," she whispered back. "I won't have my only daughter enslaved to a pack who doesn't love her or care for her. Tilly, you are special. Don't let anyone, least of all an Alpha, tell you differently. It is they who need us, not the other way around. Just take the pills and never look back." She clasped me against her in a fierce hug, one that carried the weight of a lifetime of regret.

I squeezed my eyes tightly, not wanting to believe any of this was real. Was my own mother really kicking me out of my house in the middle of the night? The only place I'd ever called home? Where I'd lived my whole life. I tried one more time, fear coursing through my veins like ice water. "But, Mama, I..."

She gave me a gentle shove toward the door. "You aren't a slave, Tilly. Don't you get it? I was wrong. This life? It's not for you. I won't let you be married off to a local pack who want nothing more than a bonus from the government and an omega for their bed. Please, baby. I can't watch them shatter your spirit. Please, just go. Run as fast as your legs will carry you and never forget how much I love you."

I staggered backward, my mother's pained words striking me with more impact than my brother's fists ever could.

She sobbed once, covered her mouth with her hand to stifle the sound, her eyes tearing up, then shut the door in my face.

For a moment I just stared at the closed door.

I can't believe it...

Then, very slowly, I turned around, gazing out over the fields of our farm. It was dark out there.

Too dark.

I wouldn't be able to see a thing if I left now, like my mama wanted me to. I was just an omega, the lowest of the low when it came to any pack's hierarchy. Could I really make a life for myself outside of the family I was born into? Outside of the pack who would soon buy me from my father?

Since the day I'd become an omega, it'd been made abundantly clear that I wasn't of use to anyone except for when I was in heat, which was something I hadn't experienced yet.

Thank the gods.

My mother's words rang in my ears, and I tried *so* hard to cling to them over the rhetoric my fathers had recited all my life. Because here I was, outside in the cold, all alone, and I had nothing but my mother's stolen or hoarded funds in my pockets and her full blessing to run. To bail out of this town on swift feet and make a life for myself.

For years, I'd been told I was good for nothing. I was destined to be yet another pack's slave. But now my mother was telling me something else. In fact, she was putting her life on the line for me. Her hope carried the rebellion and love of a mother who had suffered and didn't want to see the same cruel fate dealt to her only daughter.

When my fathers and brothers find out I'm gone... If they discover that it was her who helped me...

My throat tightened as fear threatened to freeze my muscles. Years of trained obedience had me almost bolting back inside my family's tiny farmhouse, but I fought the urge. My mother had put herself in mortal danger for me. If I ignored her plight and returned to my bed, to the destitution of my tiny room, all her courage would have been for nothing. I'd be destroying not just her wishes and hopes and disregarding her wisdom and care, I'd also be rejecting the only chance I had.

And she's right... she has to be.

She'd lived this life, which meant she knew all too intimately what my future held if I remained here. I would be sold off to a pack, today most likely, and if she didn't want that for me, then I had to run.

My eyes shimmered with tears as I faced the dark. I loved my mother more than anyone in the world. She'd always protected me and whispered words of love and support in my ears—when my fathers weren't looking, of course. She'd done and said enough on my behalf over the years for me to know that when she said *run*, I needed to run.

The first step was almost impossibly hard. My breath felt frozen in my lungs, making my body scream in pain as my legs trembled beneath me. But the next step came easier, and the fear I'd coveted for so long soon morphed into something else. Something strange and new. A bubbling feeling in my belly that I couldn't quite place.

I took another step into the darkness, followed by another. With each step, my eyes adjusted to the darkness. Above my head, like a curved blade in the sky, a half-moon cast just enough light to reveal the shapes in the gloom ahead.

Come on. You can do this!

For my mother and for my future, I bolstered my own courage, donning it like an armored blanket. I knew this yard and our long road. I also knew how far away town was. I'd walked this dusty track so many times, I knew every pothole and large tree.

No thanks to my brothers.

They often made me walk, forcing me out of the car and onto the street whenever the mood struck. To punish me for some transgression, or to simply entertain themselves, it had never mattered, until now. The first bus to the city would arrive at exactly 6am.

I can make it!

With my heart on my sleeve and a belly full of chaotic, anxious butterflies, I started running. And didn't look back.

CHAPTER ONE
TILLY

My bags were packed with everything I owned, and my last paycheck was cashed and tucked away neatly inside my wallet. It was time to move again, and I hated to admit it, but it was getting easier. I had my exit strategy down to a science, but this time, I was going farther than the state line. I needed to get far, far away from the latest pack I'd been dating.

I'd had three goes at the whole true scent match thing, and every time I'd upended my world for a pack of Alpha-holes, their true intentions had soon become clear. I'd broken up with my pack last night, and even though they hadn't believed me, I was deadly serious. I'd already given work my notice and had a new prescription for heat suppressors despite the fact they made me feel like shit, and would fill it as soon as I could. I didn't like being on them, but at least I'd be in full control of myself once more.

No stupid hormones or baser instincts were going to control me and what became of my future. Being in heat was the most intense feeling I'd ever known, as well as the scariest. Most omegas turned into sex-starved lunatics when in heat, and even though I hadn't yet reached that point, I had no intention of ever doing so. The last thing the wrong mates wanted to do was satisfy you.

The last pack I'd dated had used my needs against me, making me beg for the one thing I needed. *Them.* And after it was all over, I'd still felt empty and alone. I wouldn't do it again, I'd decided. My mom was obviously wrong. There was no such thing as a true scent match… not with an Alpha, anyway. All the men I had the misfortune of meeting were seemingly natural born assholes. The best thing I could do now was to stay on my suppressors and try to create a life without a pack.

And if I ever did happen to find a decent beta in future who didn't just treat me like a pretty object to dominate, then we'd mate and live happily ever after, without the true scent match. I didn't care about all that anymore. There was just too much pain and risk involved in continuing my search. All I wanted, moving forward, was to find someone who'd love me and treat me as well as I treated them. I didn't need fairy tales anymore, just a real sense of connection, tenderness, and safety.

That'd be more than enough.

My phone chimed with my alarm, startling me from my thoughts, and I grabbed it up to swipe the screen closed. My ex-pack of Alphas would be getting off work in a few hours, and I needed to be gone before they got home.

Time to go.

I zipped up the same tote bag I always traveled with, the one my mom had sent me off with all those years ago. I hadn't seen her since that cold morning on my eighteenth birthday, and I still didn't have any idea if she was okay.

Had my brothers come looking for me when they'd woken up and found me gone? Or had my fathers been mad that I'd left? Had they punished her?

Probably…

With a heavy heart and a throat thick with emotion, I grabbed the winter coat my mama had given me that night, an item of clothing I would never part with for as long as I drew breath. It had saved me from freezing to death on more than one occasion, and if I closed my eyes tightly and breathed in the interior of the coat, I could still feel her love wrapped around me. My heart ached.

Finally packed, I headed out the door of my tiny apartment. I'd lived above the bakery in town for a year now, and although it was warm and cozy, it was time to go. I'd been *so* close to moving in with my demanding pack, even giving notice to my landlord. Thank goodness they'd shown their true colors just before I'd made the move. I'd had no choice but to break up with them.

The keys to my old car felt heavy in my pocket. My pack, the one I'd been dating for six months, had bought it for me as a gift. It wasn't impressive, and to be honest, it didn't even run that well… but it was a car. My very first. It would get me to the next town over, or the one after that. That's all I needed. I'd become a pro at starting from nothing, and I'd do it again.

I'd moved three times since that first night, each time traveling further away from my hometown. But I'd been limited by bus routes back then. Now, I had a car. Sure, she was an old beater that'd seen better days, but she'd get me to the next leg on my journey. Where was I going to end up? God only knew.

To a true scent match. That's where you're going.

I shook my head in denial, grimacing at the memory of my mother's voice. It rang in my ears, so familiar yet so distant.

I don't think it exists, Mama. And I think I'm done trying.

Pulling the keys from my pocket, I pressed the button that opened the faded red Beetle. I'd joked with my most recent pack that they'd gotten me something old and red just so they would always know where I was at all times. You could hear me coming from miles away.

They hadn't laughed in response, nor had they defended their position. That's when I'd known that their level of *love* for me was unacceptable. I was nothing but a possession to them. Something to show off to their friends, to control, and destroy if they saw fit. I'd seen the red flags, but ignored them out of desperation and loneliness.

The fact that the government had recently doubled the financial incentive to the packs to mate and breed an omega had also made it pretty clear to me where I stood.

"Let's go, little ladybug," I said to my car as I opened the door that groaned with the movement. The old seat squeaked as I jumped in, anxious to get on with my escape. "You only have to survive one more trip, okay? Let's go get you some gas." I had cash in my pocket for fuel and food, but I was also grateful for the savings I had stashed away in my bag. Ever since I'd left my family home that night, I made sure to have cash on me at all times. I never wanted to be caught without. Never wanted to feel completely powerless and out of control.

So, I'd worked as much as I could, waiting tables and babysitting for beta working women. I made sure I didn't rely on my pack for financial support, which was *always* against their wishes. Every pack I ever dated had wanted me to immediately quit my job and move in with them, giving them all the control on a silver platter.

My recent pack was no different and had been begging me to move in with them for six months. They hadn't known I had savings stashed away so that I could leave at any time, and I never told them. Despite what everyone thought about an omega's place in the world, I promised myself I wouldn't end up like my mother—penniless, and with no other choice but to remain trapped and beholden to the men who owned me.

Even the very fact that my omega price from the government went straight to my pack and not me or my babies was proof of a system that was designed to reward only men from the outset. The game was rigged, and I, for one, sure as hell did *not* want to play.

With a deep breath, I slid the key into the ignition and turned it. The old engine coughed and spluttered for a gut-wrenching moment but soon jolted to life. One day, I'd get myself a good car. A nice car. Something that I'd proudly transport my babies around in. When I had a man who loved me.

One day... maybe.

I drove to the far side of town and stopped in at the last gas station on the highway. After filling up the fuel tank and getting a carload of snacks, I gave the town a final *goodbye* before I got back into the car. "Time to see where this road will take us," I announced to my little red bug.

The engine took another moment to turn over, but we were soon on the road again. I grabbed some pop and sighed at the satisfying sound of the hiss upon opening the bottle. "So good," I groaned as I drank some of my favorite, *Pepsi Max*. My last pack hadn't *let* me drink soda or even eat a snack they hadn't first approved. I'd lost fifteen pounds against my better judgement—because it's what they demanded of me. And truthfully, I didn't really even have the extra to lose, so I was on a health and weight gain journey now. I was going to do what was right for me.

Fuck them. Like seriously... fuck them.

I continued along the highway toward the state line, stopping only once for more fuel, and just kept going north. I had no idea where I was heading and didn't care. My old packs were all behind me now, and I wouldn't and *couldn't* look back.

None of the packs I'd broken up with had taken the news well. And if the promise I'd made to my mother hadn't been ringing in my ears, I might have stayed, and the cycle of omega abuse would have continued. But she'd told me to find a true scent match. To find men who loved me. And so far, I hadn't, so I'd kept trying... but each break-up had ultimately been the same.

It was almost like they'd each read passages out of the *Narcissist's Handbook*. Every single time, they'd told me I'd never find another pack. That I was ugly, ungrateful, and that I wouldn't survive without them. They'd been spiteful and cruel, then all had started begging within a day of my leaving.

Each time, I'd walked away, only to find another pack pursuing me within days. Mom had said that it was the men who needed us, not the other way around. And the longer I lived the single, omega life, the more I realized just how right she was. They were like the vampires, and we the blood they craved. Not to mention the house slaves, sex slaves, and breeders they wanted!

They needed us, but if we ever realized it as a whole omega collective and did something about it, the tables would turn. Omegas everywhere would wake up and leave their abusive packs for lives of freedom and independence. The whole world would collapse into chaos, falling like a house of cards, or so the soul-sucking *vampires* believed.

So, the world of men ruled with an iron fist, but it was not going to keep me ensnared for very long. I'd never stay with a man who ruled with hate and control. I refused. I could take care of myself, and I'd accept nothing less than a man who wanted to make my life better.

Not fucking worse.

Above, the skies had turned grey, and it began to rain. It was close to dinner time now and it would be too dark to drive for much longer. I wasn't afraid of the dark, not anymore, but I *was* also running out of food and I wasn't willing to let my body weight drop any more than it already had. I couldn't allow myself to get weak or fall prey to sickness and if I let myself get frail, that's exactly what was going to happen.

"Crap." I turned my windshield wipers on as a sprinkling of rain turned into a determined downpour. I needed to stop somewhere safe for the night. A large sign on the side of the highway told me there was another small town up ahead.

Fifty-two miles.

I frowned. That was a bit far, and I didn't dare push this car above sixty, so it would be an hour at least until I found the motel. And by then it would be fully dark, but what choice did I have?

I can't turn back. I won't.

I grabbed the last half bite of my *Twinkie* and threw it in my mouth.

Okay, keep it together, girl.

It was only one more hour of driving. I could do that. We'd go slow and steady if we had to. Why worry now? I'd already come so far. Cranking the music on my stereo, I started singing to fill the deafening silence around me. Maybe I should make it a personal rule to not even try to date another man for a year or so? That way I could save some money, buy a proper, reliable car and even go to a doctor to get a prescription for some of the new hormone suppressors available. Ones with less side effects would be amazing.

Despite the anxiety swirling in my gut, I grinned as the sun set on my first day of freedom. I'd done it again. A clean break. I'd be okay. I'd only stop for one night then keep on going, putting as much distance between me and my ex-pack as possible.

That's a good plan.

After everything I'd been through so far, surely things couldn't get any worse. My days of peace and safety were ahead of me. They had to be.

CHAPTER TWO
TILLY

Between the singing and reminiscing to keep my spirits up on the drive, the town came up faster than I anticipated. With no small amount of relief and happiness, I was soon following road signs directing me toward the *Star Inn*. The rain was really coming down hard, and as I parked and got out of the car, I realized the wind had a bitterly cold bite to it. There was definitely snow on the horizon.

Hopefully, I can get out of this town and find the next city before it hits!

The last thing I wanted was to get stuck in another tiny town and fall prey to the habits of my past. Resolute, I grabbed my mama's coat and pulled it on over my shivering body. "Brrr…" My teeth chattered. Losing that extra body fat certainly hadn't been good for my prospects of surviving the winter alone either.

A feeling of dread struck me as I stood at the entrance of the check-in. The sign directly above my head read 'Rooms Available' in bright blue neon lights, but that didn't necessarily mean anything for me. I could only cross my fingers that this town wasn't backward about renting rooms out to un-mated omegas. I'd come across one of those prejudiced innkeepers before, which had resulted in me sleeping in a cold, hard-tiled public bathroom overnight, riddled with anxiety and fear.

It was not a night I was eager to repeat. When you're on your own, you learn quickly not to take safety for granted.

But at least I have my car now.

It was warm and lockable, and I'd thrown a pillow and a spare blanket in the back weeks ago for moments exactly like that. It was always a good idea to have a back-up plan anyway, even if I did secure a room for the night. You could never be too careful.

Preparing myself for the conversation ahead, I inhaled deeply to settle my nerves and sighed, a feeling of warmth flooded my chest. A heavenly scent filled the air, familiar and comforting like fresh baked apple pie and warm, smooth, creamy custard, one of my favorite aromas.

Maybe they have an onsite cook as well?

That would be amazing! I'd love a real, home-cooked meal before bed, especially on a night like tonight. There was nothing quite like four safe walls, a bed, and a full belly to support a good night's sleep. As soon as I opened the door, the fragrance of baked goods hit me so hard, my mouth watered, and I had to swallow quickly before greeting the woman behind the counter. She looked to be about fifty years old, and obviously a beta. Was she the one responsible for my now rumbling belly?

"Good evening." She beamed at me in warm welcome. "How can I help you?"

Shuffling my feet, I grimaced and toyed with my keys. "I'd like a room just for the night," I said as I stepped closer. "I was planning on crossing the state line tonight, but the weather seems to have other plans."

She smiled kindly as her keen gaze drank me in from head to toe. "And it's just yourself, is it?"

I nodded, holding my breath as I waited for her to give me her verdict. Would she rent out a room to a single omega, or were those extra blankets going to come in handy after all?

Her smile only broadened. "No problem at all," she assured me. "We're quiet tonight so I can give you one of our best rooms."

"Oh…" I smiled awkwardly in return. "That's lovely of you to offer, but just your cheapest is fine," I said, stepping even closer to the reception desk. "I just need a safe place to sleep. I'll be leaving first thing in the morning."

The woman chuckled and clucked her tongue. "Oh, not to worry! There's no extra charge, love. Though, we're expecting *a lot* of snow tonight, so I hope you've got chains for your tires if you're hoping to keep driving tomorrow."

"Snow chains?" I repeated.

Damn.

I hadn't even thought about them. With a flustered smile, I licked my lips and reached into my purse. "I'm sure I'll be fine," I said quickly. "Is it okay if I pay for the room with cash?"

"It's preferred," she laughed good-naturedly, typing on her computer before swiping a card through the machine and naming her price. "You're in Room 17."

I slid the cash over the counter, pleasantly surprised by the total. Any money I could save was something to be grateful for. "Also, before I go, could I ask if your cook is still on for the night? I haven't had anything for dinner yet."

I hadn't eaten breakfast or lunch either, but the snacks from the *Sip'n'Go* had kept my sugar levels up for the day. I was still buzzing with nervous energy but starving. I felt like I could eat my weight in pie and still have room for seconds!

It won't do my figure any harm, that's for sure.

The woman, whose name was Susie, according to her nametag, gave me an apologetic smile, her brows lifted in what seemed like confusion. "We don't actually have a cook on site, I'm sorry. But I think you'll find the local diner is open late."

It was my turn to look confused. "Oh, it must be the diner I was smelling then. That apple pie on the breeze is just scrumptious. It's my favorite aroma in the whole world, actually."

The woman's mouth opened and closed but nothing came out, and her brows knitted. She looked like she wanted to say something but couldn't find the words.

"Okay, well thanks for the room," I said when nothing else was forthcoming. I grabbed my keycard and slid back toward the door, but that's when I smelled it again. The most delicious scent wafted over me, making my mouth water, and my knees shake in the strangest way. "Are you sure..." I began. And that's when I heard footsteps on the stairs—a loud, heavy man jogging down to join us.

"Hey, Mom. I—" The largest man I'd ever seen hopped off the last step, ducking his head so he didn't bop his head as he stepped into reception.

My whole body began to melt, forcing me to grab the door handle and cling to the metal anchor like a lifeline so I didn't just end up pooling into a puddle on the floor. The man, whoever he was, smelled like Heaven itself, and everything inside of me screamed "Yes! It's him. Jump on him! Now!" It took every bit of my self-preservation to pull open the door and let the freezing cold air wash over me.

The guy stopped in his tracks and smiled at me, his warm nature shining through his brilliant blue eyes like a fucking beacon on a rugged coast promising safety during a turbulent storm.

Damn it. He's so hot!

"Oh, hey," he began, "Are you—" Then he stopped again, his pupils immediately dilating as if he'd just taken a cocaine hit, and a deep rumble rolled through his chest.

My gaze shot to his mother, my breath catching in my throat and my heart racing.

What the hell is going on here?

Susie watched us with shocked but keen interest.

"Who are you?" her son growled and took a step toward me, turning what was a sweet, gruff mountain man into an obviously strong and possessive Alpha.

Crap! Oh, no! I'm not looking for another Alpha. Especially not one who smells this good.

Another rush of cold air cleared my head enough that I momentarily regained my wits. I had to get out of there. I forced myself out the door, the biting wind blasting him with my scent and sending a shiver to my very core.

The Alpha growled again, and I sensed more than witnessed his advance.

Oh... shit on a stick. Not again!

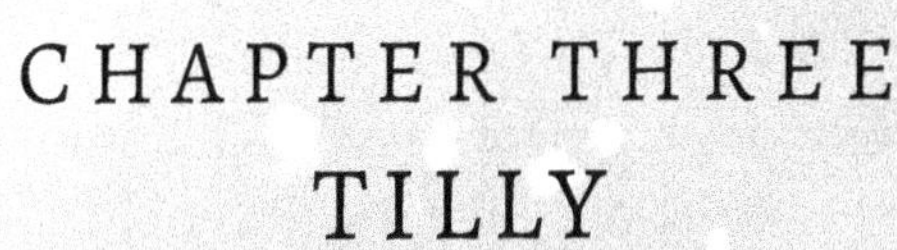

CHAPTER THREE
TILLY

I held my breath, forced a tight-lipped smile to my lips, then I ran out the door. I rushed back to my car and jumped in. *No... hell no! That was... Ah... I...*

I had no idea what that was, and I didn't want to go back inside and find out. I'd been attracted to men in the past, but my God... what was that? I wouldn't say his scent had been perfectly matched, but he was definitely scent sympathetic.

He smelled delicious! Good enough to eat.

Even his eyes were...

I shook my head and started the car. I didn't trust my own instincts when it came to men, and the last thing I needed was another money-hungry Alpha looking for an omega to service him.

No. I needed a quiet, reserved beta. Yes. Someone who could still marry me, knot me, and give me the babies I craved. That's what I needed.

Yes.

I also needed food, that was for sure. I was starving. My stomach was actually growling and hurting now. I had to get something to eat, and the lady inside said that there was an all-night diner around here.

The door to the reception area opened, and the apple pie guy stepped out, frowning at me.

"Oh, shit!" I squealed and almost dropped my car keys. Scrambling to open the car door, I managed to get the key in the ignition and tore out of the parking lot like my ass was on fire.

"Calm down, calm down," I told myself. This wasn't a bad thing. I was safe. No need to freak out. Sure, I wasn't on my heat suppressors yet, but I'd fill the prescription first thing in the morning and hopefully everything would be okay after that.

My over-reaction to him was just due to my stupid hormones. Nothing more. He was an Alpha. I was an omega. It was natural to be attracted to him, but I had to get control of myself as soon as possible.

I drove down the street, the rain pounding on my old car. The brightly lit sign of the diner was on my right, and I pulled into their drive thru with a grateful sigh.

I wound down my car window, and the drive thru window opened, a young girl with bright blue hair grinning at me. "Hello, stranger, how can I help you this evening?"

I glanced around at the brightly lit building. "This is pretty cool. I haven't seen a drive thru diner in forever."

The girl grinned. "The owner is all about keeping the big fast-food places out of town, but he wanted to offer what they did too. Convenience and good prices."

I beamed at her. "Sounds perfect to me."

"You need a menu?" she asked, already handing me a laminated sheet of paper.

I chuckled. "Yeah, just a sec." The locals probably knew the menu off by heart and ordered the same every time. I knew I'd do that if I lived here.

"The double cheeseburger with fries and a Coke. And can I get—" I scanned the dessert menu, knowing I needed more calories. "And the apple pie, with ice cream, please."

"Sure thing."

The girl was gone a bit longer than I'd expected, almost ten minutes, but when she came back to the window, my food was freshly cooked, and the smell made my mouth water.

"That smells incredible."

She grinned. "Come back for breakfast too. The egg and bacon wrap is—" She made a chef kiss move with her hand, and I couldn't help but laugh. I didn't get along with a lot of girls, since being an omega seemed to put them off talking to me, but this chick seemed really cool.

"I might just do that," I said with a smile and handed over the cash. "Thanks." I checked her name tag. "Hollie."

"So welcome," she said and handed me my change. I drove back into the rain with a full heart. What a lovely little town.

I got back to the motel in a couple of minutes, my heart beating faster and faster the closer I got. "Calm down," I repeated to myself, parking right outside my room number.

Room 17.

I looked around but couldn't see the Alpha from the reception desk. Fingers crossed he wasn't waiting for me in my room. He had access, after all, and it wouldn't be the first stalkerish thing for an Alpha to do for my attention.

There was no sign of him at the moment, and I drew a deep breath to calm my nerves. As long as I didn't see him again, I'd be fine. I was sure of it. I'd never mounted a guy before, but I'd been told it happens. When an omega finds a man scent sympathetic, which is what I thought I was to that guy, she often jumped him—quite literally. In the street, if she had to. Climbed him like a tree.

I'd never done that before. My attractions to my packs in the past had often been subtle. But that guy in the motel reception room... wow. I'd been close to behaving like a truly idiotic omega.

I needed those heat suppressors, like, *now*.

I grabbed my food and raced up to the door of the room the lady at reception had given me. Quickly sliding the keycard into the door, I pushed it open.

The scent of fresh linens hit my nose and nothing more. The Alpha guy was definitely not hiding inside. I would have been able to smell him immediately.

I shoved the door shut, embracing the sudden and immediate feeling of being safe. And clean. And alone. The room was lovely and homey. Fate, it seemed, had been kind to me tonight.

I set the food on the table and opened all the containers, inhaling the aroma before diving in. I gobbled it up so fast, my stomach immediately screamed out at me, but I was also so relieved to finally be full that I just sighed and rubbed my abs, wishing I felt like this all the time.

When I was done filling my belly, there were heaps of food left over. But round two would have to wait. I was stuffed. So instead of forcing more food down my throat, I stood up and did a small tour of the motel room, which was basically just the bedroom and a lovely white bathroom with a tub. A bathtub. I hadn't had a bath in… I couldn't remember the last one.

I rushed over and turned on the water, adjusting the temperature as it flowed, then dropped the plug into the drain. I needed a moment of pampering before I headed off on my journey again and tonight would be exactly what I needed.

I'd bathe, fill my script and my belly, then drive away.

The discomfort that came with thinking about leaving this small town was strange. But I pushed past it and stripped my clothes from my body. I didn't glance in the mirror as I passed it, not wanting to see my ribs poking out and my lack of boobs. Why the hell I'd let myself get talked into losing so much weight… I shook my head, annoyed with myself once more.

Damn Alphas.

Before I hopped in the water, I rushed back to get my untouched apple pie and a spoon, then brought it back into the bathroom. There was a small table next to the tub, which was perfect to set my dessert on.

Sliding into the bathtub was heaven. "Oh… wow." I groaned aloud as my sensitive body slid beneath the hot water, the level continuing to rise.

My nipples were tight and hard, even beneath the hot water. I ran my hands over them, gasping at the heightened response in my body.

"Damn it. I'll get the pills in the morning."

I didn't know when my next heat was due. My body was all over the place after so many years of being on and off suppressors. But it felt near. Too near.

I closed my eyes and laid my head back against the edge of the bathtub. This was just a pit stop, right? There was no reason to linger except for that diner maybe. I hadn't bought such delicious food, nor experienced such great service in… well, forever.

A deep sadness washed over me as I imagined finally settling into a town. No more moving. Making friends, girlfriends. Having a life outside of simply surviving, and running, and trying to find a mate who wouldn't treat me like I'm less than.

Not for the hundredth time, I wished I was a beta. Like Hollie or Susie downstairs. They could work and laugh and joke and marry a solitary man without anyone commenting. Their worth wasn't tied to their ability to breed or their omega price tag.

I stayed in the bath until my fingertips were wrinkled, the apple pie was gone, and my nipples were pebbled due to the cold.

Reluctantly, I stood up and hopped into the shower for a moment to warm up again, while the bath drained. Then it was time to wrap myself in my longest, warmest T-shirt, and hop into bed.

I loved sleeping alone now. The last pack I'd dated practically slept on top of me, clinging to one of my arms or legs all night, disturbing my sleep and leaving bruises when I tried to move away. But that wasn't why I loved sleeping alone.

The part that made me hate sleeping with them was that the moment they awoke, they'd recoil like I was poison, and they hadn't been attached to me like leeches all night. Pathetic. I wanted a man, or a pack, if that was possible, who adored me. Who wanted to sleep beside me and were proud to tell people that we were together.

I'd never had that, and after so many years and failed attempts to mating with a pack, I was starting to believe I never would.

CHAPTER FOUR
DAVID

*B*reakfast was done, coffee was made, and I just needed to find my keys so I could leave.

Michael stumbled out of his bedroom looking pale and exhausted.

"Long night?" I called out to him, indicating to the coffee maker on our kitchen counter. "Want a coffee?"

He nodded thanks as he sat down at the barstool, then put his head in his hands. "I just can't get that girl out of my head."

I put his black mug on the coffee machine and hit "Latte."

"What girl?" I asked, seeing my keys under a pile of mail and snatching them up. "I've gotta run."

Michael groaned and just waved at me. "I'll tell you later."

I managed to grab his mug and push it at him before I picked up my cell phone and headed out the door.

Why was I always late? Oh, that's right... I lived with my best friend, who was a man-baby, and the sheriff, who was never there. I cleaned up, did all the shopping, and made sure everyone was fed.

A pack of three Alphas was rare enough, but now I had to do everything.

"We really need an omega," I muttered to myself as I hopped into my black SUV. The vehicle I'd bought with a wife and family in mind, only to find that the woman with my scent match wasn't anywhere to be found.

The drive to my business was less than five minutes, but it was snowing heavily, so I wasn't walking, not today.

Marie had opened the pharmacy half an hour ago and set up, and once she saw that I'd arrived, she'd open the front doors for customers.

I parked in my normal spot at the back of the store, then rushed to let myself in as the snow smacked me in the face.

The moment I stepped into the store from the back, I could sense something different. I brushed off the strange feeling and walked into the pharmacy, where Marie had already let our first customer inside the front door.

My gaze was immediately drawn to the striking blonde girl standing with Marie. She was definitely an omega, too slight and pretty by half. *Wow.*

"Morning, David!" Marie called out, waving at me, then directing the girl to head in my direction.

"Hi," she said, smiling up at me as she slid a prescription across the pharmacy counter. "I'd like to fill this, please."

I grabbed the paper and saw that she wanted some heat suppressors. A new brand that was found to have less side effects. So, my instincts were correct. She was definitely an omega.

She squeaked then inhaled deeply, her face turning ghostly pale.

"Are you okay?" I asked, walking around the counter to grab her hand so she didn't fall if she fainted.

Her cheeks bloomed with heat as her body trembled under my hands. Damn, she smelled good, like vanilla and cherries.

"I've gotta go," she said, tearing her arm out of my hand and backing away. "I'll come back for that, okay?"

I nodded, my hand tingling from the contact with her skin. Her scent was amazing. Had she actually perfumed when I touched her? But that could only mean…

"Damn." I needed to call the guys. Was this the same girl Michael had talked about meeting yesterday? There was no way that we both somehow found a different omega to bond with.

Patrick, Michael, and I were a pack. That meant that she was ours. "Fuck."

I stared down at the order for heat suppressors. I had to fill this prescription, right? It was my legal and moral obligation.

Holy hell. I didn't want to do it. I wanted her to blossom under our touch. To feel the heat that was totally natural for her. But she needed to have complete control over her body and her choices.

I sighed heavily, knowing that I was going to do the right thing, even if my instincts told me to grab her and fuck her as soon as possible. And that meant despite the fact that I, an unmated Alpha, who had just found my pack's omega, I was going to give her the heat suppressors, which would stop her from bonding with us immediately.

Because it was her choice.

It would always be her choice.

I grabbed a cold bottle of water from the fridge and drank it as if I'd been a week in the desert. My throat was hot and tight, and my body was shaking, but there was excitement inside my very cells that were vibrating with happiness.

We'd found her! I'd found her! She was the one.

I filled the prescription and put it in the tub with her name on it.

Then I got back to work. The shop was full, as always, and there was always someone with a question or a new prescription to be filled.

Our omega didn't come back, as far as I knew. I spent hours watching and waiting for her, but I didn't see her or sense her. Maybe my response to her had scared her off?

After lunch, the bell above our store door rang, and Patrick walked in.

"Howdy."

I rolled my eyes at the chief of police. Who did he think he was, a sheriff in an old western? "Hey, Patrick. I need to talk to you for a sec."

The oldest Alpha in our pack swaggered his way over to me. "I need to head out. There's a report someone is stuck in the storm."

"Oh, I hope that isn't Tilly," Marie said, bustling over to join our little conversation. Everyone adored Patrick, even though he was a grump. He was mid-forties, but with age came suave confidence us young guys just couldn't emulate.

"Who's Tilly?" I asked, my heart skipping a beat.

"That young girl who came in this morning," Marie explained. "She came back for her prescription and asked me to get it for her at the front counter because you were so busy."

My groan was too loud to hide from anyone.

"What's wrong?" Marie asked.

"She's my… crap. Don't' worry. I've got to find her. Hang on. Did you say she's missing?"

"We don't know who's stranded," Patrick corrected me. "I wanted to drop by and let you know I'm heading out and my air tag is on in case you need to come and dig me out."

Marie put her hand on Patrick's arm, "You got blankets and such?"

He nodded. "Yeah, got all my gear in the truck. Gonna head out before it gets impossible to drive."

I watched my pack member head out, while I stood frozen and fuming. I turned to my lovely assistant. "Marie… you didn't come and get me for that prescription handover?"

Marie took a little step back. "It was a repeat prescription. She'd been on them for years."

"Yeah, but—"

Marie's eyebrows lowered. "But what?"

I sighed and shook my head. "If she comes back, grab me okay? Hell, if you see her in the street, tell me. I need to talk to her."

I stomped back behind the counter and got to work. I'd apologize to Marie later. Right now, I needed to stew in my own juices. I was so fucking angry at myself. I'd recognized my mate—our mate—and I'd just let her get away.

What if she was gone? What if she never came back?

CHAPTER FIVE
PATRICK

The snow fell in an almost impenetrable curtain of white. Driving out into it was a fool's errand, but I didn't have much of a choice. I'd received a call from a local farmer who'd seen a small pink or red car stuck on the mayor's private road.

Joe, the old farmer, couldn't get to his truck due to the sheer volume of snow on his property, not to mention his health issues, but I could. I strapped my best snow chains on and headed out slowly. Visibility was utter shit, but I took my time on the familiar roads and soon came upon the car Joe had been talking about. It was an old bug.

Fucking hell.

"Who the hell thought it was a good idea to drive that heap of shit around in a snowstorm?" The insanity of it begged belief. Already kitted out in my snow jacket and thermals, I grabbed my beanie and pulled it on over my graying hair. Fuck. Aging sucked, especially when you didn't have anyone to grow old with. Catching myself, I grumbled deep in my throat before returning to the task at hand.

Gazing out, I assessed the situation. The small car was blanketed heavily in snow. The windows were completely covered, as was the windshield. I couldn't see any signs of life. A familiar sense of purpose swelled within me as I grabbed my snow shovel and pushed open the door. The wind was ice-cold and felt like it went right through me, but I wasn't turning back. If there was someone in that car, they'd be dead before morning.

And I'm not having that weigh on my conscience.

I took a few trudging steps toward the vehicle, then started shoveling near the driver's side door. If I could clear enough snow, I might at least be able to get the door open.

The wind continued to howl and whipped at my face as I labored. The impossible cold was making my fingers numb, even inside my gloves. If this storm kept up for any longer, I wouldn't be able to drive the truck back anytime soon. We'd be stuck out here for hours, at the very least.

Thankfully, I was a pragmatic man and had already prepared for that eventuality. I had food, water, and heat for as long as my truck's engine kept turning over. I'd personally survived days like this one plenty of times before. I'd be lying if I said I wasn't a *little* nervous—when you lived out here you had to respect the danger posed by the elements—but I wasn't truly worried about anything other than getting this car and any potential occupants out.

Determined and unwilling to quit, my heart pumped harder as I shoveled away, fighting against the growing storm. Finally, when I'd cleared enough snow and was close enough to be able to open the car door, I swiped the driver's window clean with my thick glove.

Behind the steamy glass was the most beautiful omega I'd ever seen. Her bright blue eyes stared back at me, full of panic and fear. She was wrapped up in blankets for warmth, but I could still make out the cascade of blonde hair that flowed around her head and shoulders like a halo.

My heart practically leapt out of my chest on sight, and my will became even more ironclad. She was too young and far too stunning to be trapped in a soon-to-be metal coffin in the snow. I mentally shook away the thought, clearing my throat as I held her gaze. "Bundle up for the weather!" I shouted above the storm. "I'm getting you out of there." Despite the fact the young woman was wrapped in a blanket and coat, her lips were taking on a blue hue and visibly trembling.

Pulling open the door, I reached out my hand. "Come on."

With only a brief hesitation, she turned her whole body towards me. "Okay," she said, her voice shaky as her teeth chattered.

I shoved the car door open even wider. My hand trembled strangely as I reached to help her, but I didn't understand why.

Is this just the cold?

"What about my car?" she gasped.

This rust bucket? Seriously?

I frowned, pursing my lips before answering. "You can come back for it when the snow melts. Come on. We don't have time for this. Let's get you warm before you freeze to death."

She nodded somewhat reluctantly and grabbed her phone. Then with a heavy sigh, still wrapped up like a human burrito, she got out of the car and to her feet and waddled away from her entombed vehicle.

I took her arm so that she wouldn't fall and slammed her car door behind me. It was only a few steps or so back to my vehicle, but every foot was a battle to be won. The wind howled through the trees, blowing great gusts of snow into our exposed faces. To her credit, for a woman so slight, she didn't give up or collapse on me. Together, arm in arm, we battled the elements back to my truck, which was steadily being covered too.

Shit.

The storm was coming in harder and faster than the weather report had predicted. There really was no time. I knew only too well that even a few minutes spent exposed to conditions as extreme as this could lead to hospitalization or worse.

We have to get warm. Now!

Using the shovel, I dug my door clear as fast as I physically could, every muscle straining beneath my uniform before I managed to get it open. "Get in," I growled at the young woman who was shaking like a leaf from the cold.

She jumped into the driver's side quickly.

"Shove over," I added, even though she was already scrambling for the other side of the cabin. I hopped in after her, slamming the door. I peeled off my beanie then shook the snow from my coat. Even though we'd survived part one of this ridiculous rescue, anger rattled through me as I pulled off my coat and shoved it onto the back seat. I turned the ignition over and made sure the heater was set to high. This whole situation was a mess.

Imagine if Joe hadn't seen her! She would have died out here.

"What the hell were you thinking?" I barked. "Heading out into a storm like this?" I leaned over to grab the food and water I'd packed from the back seat and grabbed a fresh blanket for myself as well.

The girl made an awkward squeaking sound as she shivered. The outer layer of her blanket was soaked with melting snow, which wasn't helping her get warm.

A growl rattled through my chest in annoyance. "Get that blanket off. It's soaking wet. I have dry stuff for you here." I peeled off my gloves, running a cold hand through my hair, a telltale sign of my agitation. The windshield was completely covered with snow now. I couldn't even see her car through the haze of white any longer. We were all wrapped up in nature's heavy and frigid embrace. "Damn it. I don't think we're going anywhere for a while."

I couldn't look at her, so I focused on rubbing my hands together and adjusting the fans on the heat. If I did, I might strangle her for being *so* stupid and naive. When I'd cranked up the heat even further, I couldn't help myself, I finally turned to look at her. She was still wrapped in her damn wet blanket and buried so deep, I couldn't even see her face.

What is she doing?

"I told you to take that off. Do you want to freeze to death?" I snapped.

She turned slowly to look at me and her head popped up and out of the blanket like a turtle emerging from its shell. Her lips were fast taking on a shade of deep red, and her blue eyes were the brightest, most brilliant blue I'd ever seen in my life. She was the single most exquisite woman alive. My suspicions began to stir.

Oh, my fucking God... No...

"Fuck..."

Too slowly, she unwrapped herself from her blanket, struggling against the heavy, wet fabric until she was finally able to shrug it off.

The air stuck in my lungs, my heart skipped a beat, and I couldn't breathe.

Then she managed to writhe and wriggle her way out of her coat before pushing the wet mass into the backseat where my wet jacket was as well.

"Here," I said, surreptitiously gulping breaths as I handed her a dry, thick blanket. "It's a bit rough," I grunted.

"It's perfect," she said, wrapping the old woolen blanket around her body, but not before her scent hit me like a fucking tidal wave.

Like sex, sweat, and cinnamon.

"Oh... no..." I gripped the steering wheel tightly, squeezing my eyes shut as I faced the storm. "Fuck. You're an omega."

The young woman was quietly panting. I couldn't stand the way her breath whispered over her lips with the sweet sound of yearning and need. I wanted to jump out of my own truck, but there was no way I could do that and live to tell the tale. Her scent grew stronger and filled the cabin. The primal aroma made me salivate.

That means she's perfuming—*for me*—and I'm trapped here.

"Yes, I am, but..." She trailed off.

"But what?" I demanded, finally opening my eyes to turn and glare at her. "I can smell you from here, and you're..."

She was in heat. Oh, God.

How was I going to stop myself from fucking her right here in my sheriff's truck while stranded in the snow? My cock grew thick and hard in my jeans, and the pain emanating from my sac was so intense, I started to consider braving the snowstorm outside, rather than face off against the tiny blonde bombshell locked in my truck with me. I glanced back at her, hanging onto the steering wheel for dear life.

What the fuck am I going to do? Oh, fuck it....

She was even more attractive when her face was flushed red with the shade of her desire, and she'd pushed the fresh blanket down, obviously flustered. "I... left my suppressors in my car," she whispered.

I stared out the window in the direction of her car, even though I knew it was already completely obscured from view. "Too fucking late to tell me that now, sweetheart." I *knew* I sounded like an asshole—an old grump—but what was I supposed to do? Joe's farm wasn't too far away. I could make a dash for it, but she couldn't. She wouldn't make it. But could I stomach leaving her alone with my supplies?

No... I can't leave her. I won't. Fuck!

My hands were literally tingling with the need to reach out and touch her, and there was no way I could keep my eyes off her now. She was so fucking gorgeous. The curves of her flushed cheeks just begged for my lips to trail kisses along them. I could already see it... Her perfect mouth would sigh as my lips tasted her cunt for the first time. "You're unmated?" I managed to grit out.

She nodded. "Yes."

"And how old are you?"

Please be fucking legal. Please.

I'd throw myself at the mercy of the snow if she wasn't.

"Twenty-three," she answered, her voice breathy and soft.

I groaned. I was forty-five. She was young enough to be daughter.

Holy shit...

My shameless cock was so hard, it strained forcibly against my seams, threatening to tear through the very fabric of my sheriff issue denim jeans. She was shivering again, but I could see the sweat from her heat on her upper lip. "You're..." I started, each word a struggle to get out. "You smell... *really* good."

The young omega began moving in a different way. It was almost like she was swaying hypnotically to music only she could hear.

My hands dropped down to my thighs, gripping the muscles hard. I dug my fingers in, causing pain to course through my body. It was all I had, a tangible anchor to hold fast to in the storm of an Alpha-omega true scent match that was driving me fucking insane.

It seemed my rescue had no intention of holding back or fighting what nature demanded of her. Her hands wandered to her breasts, where her fingers circled her nipples absently.

I squeezed my eyes shut again in anguished frustration. It was the only way I had of blocking out the vision of how goddamn sexy she was.

Fuck!

"This isn't good," she whispered, her rock-hard nipples poking through her shirt to tease me.

"I'm aware," I groaned back.

"But I want you." she said, her lower lip trembling with desire. "I need you."

My cock practically sprung through the zipper of my pants, and my heart thundered in my chest louder than any chainsaw.

That was it. That was her consent. Her permission.

Why the hell was I trying to fight my desire for an unmated omega who was so obviously my scent match and who wanted me?

Idiot.

"Get over here," I growled, unbuckling my belt and unzipping my pants, releasing my cock from its prison of fabric.

Without another word, she shoved her pants down her thighs, taking a moment to pull off her boots before she skittered closer.

I released the lever to lean my seat back as far as it would go in anticipation, but even with that extra room, we didn't have a lot of space.

Not that it matters.

I wanted to be inside her as deeply as I could drive, as close as two people could get. I lifted my hips enough to shove my own pants down my thighs just as she threw her leg over me and slid into my lap. Her scent wafted all over me, and the growl that crawled its way up my throat was feral.

She shivered in my arms, her palms moving to trace my roughened cheeks. She clung to me like a lifeline and whimpered.

"Kiss me," I demanded, no longer able nor wanting to hold back. As she pressed her lips to mine, I grabbed her ass, hauling her against me to grind my rock-hard cock against her wet pussy. Her lips were a heaven a grouch like me didn't deserve, but I swept my tongue inside her mouth, cherishing it even more, groaning at the perfection of her taste all the while.

No one had ever kissed me *so* perfectly.

No one had ever tasted *so* sweet.

I lifted my head to break our kiss, my breathing heavy. "Tell me that you want me to fuck you."

Her sweet lips trembled as she stared at me with wide, blue doe-like eyes. "I do."

"But?" I demanded, holding her captive over my cock, but not moving an inch. I would *never* take anyone against her will, even though her heat was demanding I did.

"But… I've never felt this way before. Your smell is *so* amazing. I don't want to fight it." She dropped her head, pressing her nose against my neck before inhaling deeply.

I closed my eyes and willed myself to cling to what little self-control I still possessed. "I won't fuck you if you don't want me," I managed to get out. "We can fight the heat."

Though we'll probably die trying.

"I can get out," I told her, shaking with the effort of not surrendering to my most primal, Alpha instincts. "I can walk to the nearest farm and hunker down there. You'll be safe here without me until I come back. You have water, food, and blankets."

She made a sinfully cute yelping sound and wrapped her arms around my neck, clinging to me like limpet to a rock. And when she spoke into my ear, her breath warm against my skin, she said the words I was desperate to hear. "No… please! Don't leave me. I need you. *Please.*" She rocked her hips over me, wearing my willpower down until the head of my cock was painting her lips with my pre-cum.

"Fuck it." I swore. "I need you too. Lift your knees, beautiful. Let me get into you nice and deep."

She whimpered with need as she willfully obeyed, lifting her knees. Her wet, pink pussy smelled like caramel to my keen Alpha senses.

It was more than I could take and I groaned aloud. "I'm going to eat you out when we have more room," I growled. "You smell fucking divine."

She leaned toward the steering wheel, her back arched as she tried to ensnare my cock with her needy pussy.

I grabbed her hips impatiently and lined the head of my cock up with her slick opening. Her pussy was so hot, wet, and ready for me that I almost lost my fucking mind. Without hesitation, I captured her lips in another soul-shattering kiss of ecstasy, then greedily pulled her down onto my cock, reaching for the very heart of her with a single deep thrust.

CHAPTER SIX
TILLY

A scream of pure pleasure tore from my throat as the sheriff's cock pierced my aching, pulsing body, enflaming every inch of me with prickling heat. I hadn't even discovered the man's name, and yet he was my scent match—my Alpha. Unbelievable. I'd finally found him. I'd fulfilled my mother's deepest hope for me, and kept my promise.

I've really found him!

"Please don't stop," I begged, the fire inside my belly growing with each heart-racing moment that passed.

The sheriff groaned, then pulled me closer and buried his nose in my neck, soaking in my scent.

I panted hard, the sound of his arousal, the huskiness of his deep, gravelly voice almost too much to bear.

He growled into my ear, each word like a rumbling note of carnal promise. "I'll never stop fucking you. Never. You feel amazing." Without warning, the sheriff bit into the side of my neck like an animal and thrust up inside me.

Shock ripped me through me, warring with pleasure, as a cry spilled from my lips. Again and again he plundered me, his rhythm just perfect. His raw desire juxtaposed against his comforting, authoritative presence fed into my hunger like the most exquisite dessert, satisfying me, yet making me yearn for more.

My rescuer was hard as nails and bounced me on his cock like I was a mere doll, and I loved it. I loved that he was taking control, that he was just taking what he wanted from my body.

I hope he never stops.

I planted my feet the best I could on the seat back either side of him and tilted my hips, needing to feel him deeper. I wanted to ride him hard, but the space was so small and hot. Sweat beaded on my face and back, and yet I'd never felt so alive.

"Lift your top," he commanded, still sliding me up and down his cock, never missing a beat. "I want to suck those gorgeous tits."

I would have blushed fiercely if I wasn't so turned on. Instead of trying to process everything, I simply did as he asked. Wrangling my arms above myself, I peeled my wet top off and slipped my bra over at the same time.

"Come closer," he growled, the flames of unbridled passion flickering in his gaze with a quiet but possessive intensity.

I arched my back, offering myself up to him, craving the feel of his lips on me.

He launched forward like a starving man, suckling one tight, sensitive nipple, then the other.

My scream filled the cabin as a fresh wave of pleasure ricocheted around inside me, sending an orgasmic wave surging within my belly. Unable to deny my instincts, I tightened around him in wanting, squeezing his perfect cock. I needed him. I'd never experienced such an intense heat before, thanks to the suppressors.

I need him so badly, I feel like I could die!

The moment he released my tender nipples, I dove for his lips, grabbing his face with desperate hands before capturing his mouth in another passionate kiss. Unlike other men in my past, he didn't shy away from my kisses, which was a first for me. And it only made me love him that much fucking more.

My pussy throbbed and ached, and with every thrust inside me, the sheriff made it worse *and* better, all at once. The sensations assaulted me from all sides, filling me with a need like no other.

"Oh, fuck!" he gritted out, his breathing hot and heavy. "I'm going to blow soon, sweetheart. Your pussy is just too fucking perfect. You fit me like a glove."

Hearing those words was the single biggest turn-on of my life. Knowing that my Alpha was just as attracted to me as I was to him meant everything. Then, taking me by surprise, his cock began thickening inside of me, and there was a swelling developing at the base. "Oh fuck! The knot," I gasped, my lust-glazed eyes wide. I'd never felt it before, never known the true feeling of an Alpha knotting his omega. No one had ever been my match—until now.

I felt both terrified and elated to finally understand and feel the beginnings of my true purpose as an omega.

With a deep growl, he grabbed me and pulled me down over the substantial thickening. "You stay right where you are," he warned, his lower lip slack with desire as his gaze ravaged me alive.

I could feel the knot growing inside me all the while. Tears of joy and frustration gathered in my eyes as my belly continued to tighten, with no relief in sight. My heart raced, galloping inside my chest as ecstasy swept through me.

This is it. It's really happening!

The gorgeous, uniformed hunk who was claiming me gasped as he gripped my thighs—hard—holding me tightly against him as he stiffened inside me.

The world, like an explosion of color, seemed to erupt all around me, the beauty of our union drowning me in a tsunami of erotic pleasure and soul-deep connection. My orgasm hit hard, slam-dunking me on the reef of my desire as I screamed out to the man inside me.

My mate's roar of completion was just as loud as mine, but much deeper and carnally guttural.

Like a gloriously satisfying glitter pour, my first orgasm ended, lulling only briefly before it flowed into the next as his hot seed pulsed inside me to the rhythm of his heart. Breathless and tacky with sweat, I rode the waves of bliss like a surfer in a storm. Over and over, I shuddered and groaned, my body wracked with mind-bending pleasure. My pussy pulsed and gripped the sheriff's cock as he swelled inside me, and kept on swelling.

The sensation was too much and not enough all at once. Excruciatingly sweet and oh, so powerful. My eyelashes fluttered as my eyes rolled back, caught on the precipice of yet another wave of delirium. "Oh, God… you're knotting me!" I threw my head back as his seed continued to pulse inside me, impossibly long and perfect, hot and orgasm-inducing.

His knot swelled within me until I could no longer move up and down his cock. I was stuck, held captive by our lust and need for each other. Another orgasm hit me at the mere thought of us being so perfect together, the ripples of pleasure squeezing even harder this time. I moaned and slumped forward, digging my teeth into the sheriff's shoulder, and loving the taste of his skin beneath my lips.

"Shit," he groaned in my ear, his fingers sinking into my hips to hold me tightly.

Without a choice, I rode the waves of his release until I was spent and exhausted. I laid in his arms, shivering in the aftermath of every orgasmic crest my poor, exhausted body could wring from me.

Finally, when the sheriff's breathing evened, and the last of him filled me, I tried to raise myself up. I needed to climb off him, curl up into a ball and sleep. I craved rest in a way I never had before. I also needed to ask the gorgeous man for his name.

His fingers gripped me hard in response. "Where are you going?" he asked.

I blushed, then smiled, feeling distinctly awkward. "Ah, don't you want me to get off you now?"

He shook his head slowly. "No, I do not. And even if you wanted to, you couldn't."

I frowned at that. Was he challenging my willpower, or was there more to it? I tried again to lean away from him and felt an unfamiliar ache deep within my pussy. My breath caught in my throat, and I pushed down with my feet for leverage, but he was right—I couldn't move—we were stuck together. I swallowed hard, overwhelmed by the strange and unfamiliar feeling. "I've never... um... this is new for me," I admitted.

Oh my God... I'm being knotted! Finally, it's happened. This is what it's all about! What finding a true mate is.

He smiled very gently, the tilt of his gorgeous lips making me melt a little more. The sheriff didn't seem like a man who smiled a lot, but when he did, it lit me up to my very core. "Me too," he confided, his voice surprisingly soft. "So, let's just enjoy the moment. Come back here, baby girl." My ruggedly handsome hero coaxed me to lay my head against his chest and reached around us for a blanket. A moment later, he draped the clean, dry fabric over my back, then wrapped his arms around me.

A deep warmth settled over my soul and suddenly, I could barely keep my eyes open. I'd never felt anything like it before and found it hard to describe, even to myself. I just felt so... warm. So safe. A delicious heaviness tugged at my eyelids, beckoning me to succumb to the deep sleep that beckoned me, but I needed to ask him one more thing before I gave into oblivion. "I... I never got your name," I breathed.

He chuckled, the sound calming as his chest rumbled beneath my ear. "It's Patrick, baby. My name's Patrick."

"Patrick," I repeated, loving the way it sounded falling from my lips.

My big Alpha... my Patrick. My sheriff.

A yawn tickled up my throat, and I sighed. I had *so* many more questions I wanted to ask him, but I couldn't stay awake any longer. With a smile on my face, I let my eyes close and settled even more deeply into his strong, welcoming arms. "The sound of your heartbeat is so nice," I whispered. "It feels like home."

He relaxed back into the reclined seat. "Home. I couldn't have said it better, myself."

I sighed happily against him. His heartbeat was so steady and strong against my ear. He was big and warm, and I felt so safe, I couldn't get over it. When his arms came around me beneath the blanket and squeezed me tightly, tears welled in my eyes. I'd never known this type of protection—not from my fathers or my brothers, and certainly never from any males I'd slept with.

Is it really possible for an Alpha male to be this loving?

I smiled against my mate's strong chest. This wasn't about love. This was pure and simple physiology. He was an Alpha, and I was his omega. His omega… I could still scarcely wrap my mind around it.

My true scent match. Mama, I found him. I did it. This is real!

I snuggled into his chest and sighed again, letting my fears and reservations from the past out with my breath. No matter what was to come, I was stuck with Patrick, so I figured that I may as well try to sleep while I could and rekindle my energy.

"Sleep, baby girl," he whispered over my head and kissed my hair softly, the tenderness in his voice impossible to ignore.

Because of our clear age gap and the distinct sense of protection enveloping me, a cheeky voice inside my head whispered in return.

Night, Daddy.

With a final smile against him at the amusingly taboo thought, I fell into a deep, peaceful, and dreamless sleep.

WHEN I AWOKE NEXT, I wasn't even sure how much later it was. My face was still firmly plastered to the sheriff, his steady heartbeat filling my ears like a delicious lullaby. He was snoring softly, and as I lay there awake but unmoving, I absorbed every little moment of my first true knotting. I didn't need anyone to tell me just how precious and momentous an occasion it was. I felt like I'd been waiting all my life for it!

The other packs I dated never had this sort of reaction to me. They'd wanted me physically, but the attraction was nothing compared to what I'd just experienced. And they'd never ever held me after the sex was done and they'd had their fill of me. Never.

Speaking of sex...

Biting my lip, I shifted slightly in his lap, feeling the ache of having been stretched too far around his knot. But he was no longer swollen, and I could lift up. When I dared to try my luck, he slipped out. The immediate sense of emptiness from his absence was horrible, but there was no way to fix that. I felt incredibly satisfied, so perhaps I hadn't gone into heat the way I assumed.

Maybe this is what it's like when you find your true scent match?

All of it was new to me, so I just couldn't know. As I tried to move back to the passenger seat, I felt immediate resistance.

Patrick's hands clamped down on my thighs, his fingers digging into my flesh. "Where are you going?" he asked. He looked and sounded almost panicked.

Licking my lips, I allowed myself to slide back down, letting our flesh meet once again in a sizzle of connection that shocked me. "Nowhere," I said honestly. "I was just going to move back to my seat, that's all."

He frowned. "No. Stay here. Please."

The "please" hit me *hard*. The words were nothing more than a genuine and heartfelt request, but at the same time, I felt like I couldn't say no if I wanted to. The connection I felt was frightening in its intensity, but at the same time, it was yet another strange and foreign feeling. He had control, and so did I. There was no anger or venom, no threat or fear of harm. Just a bond that felt balanced and natural.

"Okay," I agreed, and his shoulders immediately relaxed. He was still wearing his sheriff's shirt, and I found my fingers dancing along the buttons, opening them one after another as I went.

"What are you doing?" he asked, glancing down at my busy fingers.

"Can I just… touch you?" I asked, already opening his shirt wide so I could slide my fingers through the hair on his chest. "Do you mind?"

He shook his head but didn't speak, his posture relaxing immediately beneath me.

I'd never felt welcome to explore the men of my packs in a leisurely, non-sexual way. If I ever kissed any of them or tried to show some small level of affection, it was taken as an invitation and a prelude to sex. Which soon meant that if I wasn't in the mood, I learned not to touch them at all. That sort of attitude and those assumptions bred hostility on both sides.

This is so much better.

Patrick stirred beneath me, and yet he wasn't trying to actively seduce me or take me by force, which was a rather heady feeling. I dug my nails into his flesh, kneading his pecs, which were thick and strong with muscle.

"Tell me your name," he said, his tone dark and aroused.

"Tilly," I said. "It's short for Matilda, but no one calls me that."

"I like it," he grunted appreciatively.

I glanced up at him through my eyelashes, feeling my own arousal rising again. He smelled so good, like vanilla, but also somehow like fresh burnt sugar. Toffee.

Just delicious.

He coughed to clear his throat, still holding me close. "And where did you come from, Matilda?"

The way he used my full name made me shiver. I loved the way he said it, the way it sounded falling from his lips. He made me feel like a whole new woman, which was exactly what I needed. To be remade into the person I'd always wanted to be. "From Birchwood originally," I answered. "But I haven't been back there in years. I don't want to ever go back."

"So, when I found you… you were just passing through?" He gasped as my fingernails scraped over his nipples, but he still didn't move to do anything more.

"I was." I nodded, mentally noting my use of the past tense.

"You'll come back to town and stay with us?" His words were a command, and yet his tone turned them into a question. He left me grace to refuse. But how could I?

I bit my lip and sucked in a deep breath. "Who's… *us?*"

"My pack," he said, his gaze boring into mine.

I closed my eyes and nodded. Of course, he had a pack. He was an Alpha. But who were they? "Who exactly is in your pack?" I ventured, remembering my body's response to the two other men I'd met just yesterday and earlier in the morning. "They don't happen to work at the motel or the pharmacy by any chance, do they?"

The sheriff's eyes widened as big as saucers, and his eyebrows sprung up in shock and surprise.

Patrick's reaction instantly confirmed my suspicions, and even though my heart raced, his expression was the most charming thing I'd ever seen.

CHAPTER SEVEN
MICHAEL

"They're just ahead of us, I think," I said, pointing out Taylor's road as David and I slowly drove through the snow in a minivan.

"I can't believe that idiot turned off his phone," David grouched with a shake of his head while navigating the perilous landscape.

It had been four long hours since Patrick had taken off from the pharmacy to find and rescue a damsel in distress. If it was by any chance the same woman I'd met last night, there was a distinct possibility that Patrick had sensed something special about her too. "There's the truck!" I said, pointing again when it came into view.

"And a small red car," David added, gesturing with his chin. The car was visible beneath the melting snow, but only just. "I hope he got her out of there."

I grunted in acknowledgement but didn't talk. As a pack of three Alphas, we'd been told repeatedly over the years that we'd never find an omega to suit us. We were apparently all too strong, far too much for one woman to handle. But their negativity hadn't stopped us from hoping. From dreaming.

If this girl is ours...

I caught myself mid-thought and grimaced, sucking in a deep

breath as I tried not to think about what it would mean. But one thing was for certain—if she was, our lives would never be the same again.

David pulled up next to the sheriff's truck and switched off the ignition, unbuckling himself.

I followed suit, opening the van's door before stepping out into the icy white world around us. We'd brought my mom's minivan, full of supplies and blankets, just in case. A pack had to have each other's backs, after all. "Hello?" I called out, pressing my gloved hand to the truck's window and brushing the snow from the glass so I could see inside. The scene that revealed itself to me was like something from a movie and took my breath away.

The gorgeous little blonde I'd met briefly at the motel last night was straddling Patrick, her hands all over him. I could have sworn that the sheriff blushed upon seeing me, but that could have been from the cold. It did have a tendency to pinken up the nose and cheeks. I cleared my throat, even though they wouldn't have been able to hear me, then tapped on the glass. "Do you guys need any help?" I said, raising my voice to be heard.

He nodded and pulled the blankets up and around the girl even more tightly. "You got a shovel?" he asked.

I gave Pat a thumbs up and went back to the minivan, a sharp pang of jealousy making my insides ache as I trudged. "They're okay!" I called into the van, toward David. "It looks like the sheriff's already mated with her."

"He *what?*" David exclaimed as he hopped out of the driver's side and trekked through the snow and around the van to see for himself. When he turned back to me, his lips were tilted up in a smile. "Well, at least we were right about her being our mate then," he said, referring to our earlier conversations in Patrick's absence.

I grabbed the shovel and shrugged at him, then began moving the snow around the truck one big shovel load at a time, focusing my attention on the stubborn white sludge. "Aren't you even a bit mad?" I asked.

David laughed. "Are you kidding me? If we're lucky and this is a true scent match for us, then we've literally got forever, Mike. Don't stress out about who got to her first. It doesn't matter—first or last. As long as we're all together, who gives a shit?"

But I was the one who met her first.

Since then, I'd dreamed about her, the scent of her perfection tickling my nose since the moment she'd stepped into my mom's office. Regardless of how I felt, I didn't bother to give voice to my anger any further. Instead, I worked doggedly around the truck to free the tires from the snow's grasp.

Patrick turned the key the moment we stood back to check out our handiwork, and the big truck's engine roared to life. He rolled down the window, while the girl struggled under the blankets on the passenger side, probably trying to get her clothes back on.

"Do you want to follow us home?" David asked from beside me.

Pat shook his head ever so subtly. "Matilda wants to go back to the motel."

My heart clenched, and my insides flip-flopped in panic at his words.

She doesn't want to come home with us? Why?

Suddenly, her head popped up from her sweater and blanket, and she stared straight at me.

My stomach lurched in recognition. It was definitely her, all glistening, gorgeous skin, bright blue eyes, and luscious, long blonde hair. I went to walk away, but her window slid down, and I automatically found myself walking around to her side to hear what she had to say.

"Hey." She smiled with recognition that made me ridiculously happy.

I nodded back at her, my hands stuffed deeply into the pockets of my jacket. "Hey." I couldn't help but inhale her scent as I stepped closer. Mixed with the thick smell of sex, it wafted from the air within the truck's cabin. Somehow, it wasn't the turn off I thought it would be. It was quite the opposite, in fact. I stifled a groan of desire. She was in heat.

Matilda curled her fingers over the open window. "Do you think your mother would mind if I stayed in my room at the motel a bit longer?" she asked with the distinct tone of hope in her voice.

I shook my head and choked out my words, barely able to control myself. "No, not at all. That'll be fine," I assured her.

She smiled in relief. "Thank goodness," she said, her warm breath whirling in the chilly air between us.

I fought the urge to reach out and touch her, to graze that lovely skin with my own. And God, I yearned to kiss her *so* badly, it felt like I might explode. But this wasn't the time or place. This was a rescue mission, not the scene of a backseat orgy. I huffed a heavy sigh. Perhaps it had simply been too long. Was I just desperate to fulfill our wildest dreams? Was I overreacting?

Maybe she isn't our true scent match. Maybe she's just Patrick's.

The thought made my heart sink.

Matilda's gaze kept sliding over to the half-buried red car.

I glanced that way too, realizing that she was probably worried about someone smashing into it or something. I certainly didn't want that for her or whoever might be unfortunate enough to find it buried in the snow. "If you throw me your keys, I'll drive your car back after we dig it out. You need to stay warm and get home." At least I could be useful.

"Really?" Her voice perked up even more, and she reached out for my hand, her big blue eyes finding mine.

I offered my hand to her, my entire world narrowing down to a single moment. "Yeah, of course," I said. "We're here to help."

She grabbed my fingers hard.

My skin tingled on contact, and I gritted my teeth behind my lips, longing for more of her touch.

"Oh, thank you!" she exclaimed. "The keys are still in the car. But everything I own is in there. So, if you could save it, I'd really, *really* appreciate it."

My cock hardened at the recognition of the promise I heard in her voice. "It's no trouble," I managed, all but chaffing at the proverbial bit. I had to stop overthinking this and trust my instincts. I felt what I felt, and that was that—there was no denying it.

Patrick chuckled behind her. "How about I get Matilda some food, and we'll meet you guys back at the motel, pack member?"

I glanced up at Patrick's steady gaze full of understanding and an undertone of amusement. He'd never referred to me in such a manner, but I appreciated it now. We *were* a pack, after all. We had been for almost a decade.

I looked back at Matilda, who didn't so much as flinch at the mention of our pack.

Has Patrick already filled her in?

"Okay," I said, referring to his plan, then took a step back. "We'll meet you back at the motel."

Matilda, whose name didn't suit her completely, in my opinion, squeezed my hand once more, then slid the window back up. She shivered even in the warmth of the cabin and rubbed her hands together before breathing into them.

I tapped the top of the truck to signal that David and I were out of harm's way, and that Patrick should get going. A rumbling moment later, they were headed off to safety.

I picked up the shovel and made my way over to the small red car.

"Do you seriously want to dig this out now?" David asked, staring at the pile of snow that had been dumped on top of the Beetle.

I shrugged. "Why not? We don't want it to cause a traffic jam after the snow melts. If there's an accident, Pat will be called away again."

Not to mention, I didn't want our mate to lose every possession that she owned in this world. We didn't have a lot of theft in our town, but that didn't mean we could guarantee someone wouldn't steal something. It wasn't worth the risk, especially if we wanted to make her feel at home and happy.

"Okay. Whatever you say," David said with a glint in his eye.

Together, we dug in and luckily for us, the snow came away in huge chunks, sloughing off the vehicle and making it easier to move. Soon, we'd freed the little red car in no time.

"See you back at the motel?" David called, heading back to my mother's minivan.

"Yep." I opened the driver's side door of the Beetle and stared down at the tiny space with a grimace of uncertainty. I was almost six feet six. I was never fitting into this car.

Unless...

I reached down and slid the seat back as far as it would go, but still wasn't convinced there was enough space for me.

Maybe I should just get David to drive it...

But then the smell hit me—her scent—my mate's scent. It changed my mind instantly. There was no way I was letting David drive this car. I slid one leg in, then kind of shoved the rest of myself inside like a clown car. I dropped the back of the seat further and pretended my head wasn't hitting the roof. Cramped as I was, I managed to fit myself in and shut the door. Then I inhaled, slowly. "Oh. My. God." If this was just *scent sympathetic*, I'd bite my own ass. She smelled incredible. Every fiber of the car was infused with it.

I grabbed a sweater from the passenger seat and put it to my face, glad no one was around to witness me sniffing her clothes like a weirdo. I'd dreamed of my omega for so long... I couldn't believe we'd finally found her. The realization made my heart burn with joy, and my soul sing.

David had already driven off, so I reached for the keys and turned them in the ignition, hoping the engine would start. If it didn't, I'd have to call David back to pick me up again. The car vibrated and rattled, the engine struggling to turn over in the bitter cold. I waited, counted to ten, then tried again. This time, mercifully, the engine sputtered to life, and I threw it into reverse before the engine could die on me.

It rolled backward, and I followed the tracks made by David's car to keep the little red bug from getting bogged down. Without incident, I managed to drive it slowly back to the motel. I needed to get the car dry and warm, or everything was going to freeze again and the engine would seize. Diesels couldn't take the cold for long periods of time.

I shook my head as I pulled the car into an undercover parking spot at the motel. The little car was *so* small and old. It was hard to imagine any pack allowing her to drive this unreliable thing, let alone buying it for her. Hopefully, she'd got it for herself, or I'd have some heads to crack! My knees sounded like popcorn as I pushed open the door and hastily untangled myself in an effort to get out of the car, tripping and almost falling on my ass in the process.

David's laughter from behind me had me scowling over my shoulder. "You didn't think about the size of the car when you offered to drive it back for her, huh?"

Grabbing the battery tender we kept for guests with similar cars, I connected it and growled at him in annoyance. "Not all of us went to college for eight freaking years," I retorted. "Let's go."

I grabbed the duffle bag from the backseat of her car.

David grinned in amusement as he snatched up a blanket and a pillow. Then he stopped laughing and groaned, his eyes widening as he glanced down at his crotch in wonder as her scent washed over him. "What in the..."

"Yeah, I *know*," I said, heading for the stairs. I was hard as a rock again and walking up the stairs was going to be fucking uncomfortable. But with every step I took, I was one step closer to my scent match... So, with renewed determination and no small measure of pig-headed stubbornness, I walked on, David not far behind me.

CHAPTER EIGHT
TILLY

The room didn't feel right any longer. I'd been happy enough with my accommodations last night, but now—and I couldn't put my finger on how or why—it just wasn't how things should be. It was too bare... too empty. "Can I have your jacket?" I asked Patrick suddenly.

He frowned at me, tilting his head curiously. "My sheriff jacket?"

I bit my lip and nodded, hoping against hope he wouldn't deny me. He probably needed it for work tomorrow, but I *needed* something that smelled like him. It wasn't a choice or want—I had to have his scent.

He didn't ask further questions after that, he just shrugged out of the jacket and held it out to me, the smallest hint of a smile quirking the edges of his lips.

My heart fluttered, and I hurried over to grab the soft leather. I held it up to my face and inhaled deeply before moving back to the bed. It occurred to me that I also didn't have enough pillows or blankets. The bed just wasn't comfortable or soft enough for my liking.

Not yet, anyway.

But as I laid the jacket on my pillow, the rich scent of Patrick filled my senses all over again, I took another deep breath, then sighed.

Even with just the addition of one piece of clothing, the space looked and felt better somehow. I couldn't explain it, and there was no time to ponder it further because the door to my motel room opened, and I glanced up.

Michael stood in the doorway carrying my bag. "Hey again," he said, raising his free hand briefly in greeting.

"Oh, thank you!" I cried, running over to him. With all my focus on decorating my space, I'd completely forgotten about everything from my little red car. My clothes, photos, cash… everything was there.

He saved it all!

As soon as I got within arm's length, I reached out for my bag and inhaled the air around us. "Damn, you smell incredible too." I should have stepped away like I had the first time I'd smelled Michael that first night in the motel reception room. Instead, I threw caution to the wind and stepped closer, raising myself up on my tiptoes so that I could touch him. I pressed both hands against his pecs and stuck my nose into the crook of his neck, breathing deeply. "Just like apple pie and cinnamon." I sighed anew. He smelled like comfort. Like a home I'd never known.

I can't run away now.

The need no longer existed. I didn't have to keep moving, not when I knew this pack was mine and these men were mine. Getting stuck inside that truck with Patrick during the blizzard had broken down all the walls I spent years carefully constructing around myself. Now, I had the chance to start fresh. A chance to learn to love and be loved the way I should have always been as an omega.

Michael dropped my bag and groaned, his eyes flashing with restrained desire. "What are you doing?" he asked.

I glanced up at him, confused.

What does he mean? I'm not doing anything.

But my hands were! They were kneading his flesh and gliding over his erect nipples through his sweater. And that wasn't the only erection in my vicinity. My hips swayed of their own volition to the music playing inside my head, grinding against the bulge in his jeans. "You're so tall," I whispered.

"Boys, you're back," a familiar female voice said from behind David.

I jumped in surprise, startled by the presence of another woman, and stumbled back toward the bed.

Michael stepped deeper into the room and sat down on the nearest chair. We shared an embarrassed look, as if we'd been caught out, before glancing back at David and Susie.

"Shut the door. It's still blowing a gale outside," she said.

David shut the door behind them, his gaze following my movements without comment or greeting.

"Hmm..." I nodded to myself in thought, sliding onto the bed and grabbing for a pillow. I had the strangest desire to build a nest, something I had never experienced before. But I knew what this was. I needed somewhere to fuck and smell my mates while I slept. I was finally nesting, and it was the weirdest fucking thing ever.

"David said you might be wanting to stay for a few more days?" Susie ventured.

I nodded again, half lost to my own little world. "Yes, I think so. Perhaps longer, if that's all right?" I answered.

Michael's mom glanced at where I was perched on the bed, then around to Patrick, David, and Michael. The penny seemed to drop. Her cheeks blushed a soft pink as she stumbled over her words. "Oh... Is this... Are you... I think I interrupted something just now. I'm *so* sorry."

"It's okay," I reassured her. "I mean, I don't really know what's happening, to be honest, beyond the obvious. It's all new to me."

She gave me the kindest, most genuine smile. "Well, maybe you all need to sort that out. Although, their house is probably the best place for your nest, dearie. They have a large basement and a spacious loft, too."

I looked around at the pillows and blankets, embarrassment searing a path of heat over my cheeks. "Oh, I wasn't... I didn't..." It was my turn to trip over my own tongue it seemed.

"You boys need to take her home with you," she said, only she wasn't addressing me now, which made it even more embarrassing.

I'd never wanted to be an out-of-control omega, one whose hormones dictated her every move.

How ridiculous. I'm so much more than my body!

"She wants to stay here, Susie," Patrick told the motel owner firmly, his deeply timbred voice making my insides clench with wanting. "She's not comfortable moving in with us immediately, which I respect."

Well said, Daddy.

"She has to," Susie told the sheriff, not backing down an inch. "You're a true scent match for each other, correct?"

Patrick straightened even taller, hesitating for only a moment before nodding in concession. "Yes, ma'am."

"Then you need to take her home. Allowing her to set up a nest here will cause problems with her heat, and if she gets pregnant, she won't want to leave here at all for at least the next year or two. Do you all want to live in a motel for that length of time?"

"Ah…" Pat pursed his lips and the three men glanced at each other, confused as to what to do.

I cleared my throat, and everyone turned to look at me. I focused on Susie, rather than the men I so desperately wanted to mount like a bitch in heat. "How do you know that, Susie? You're not an omega."

She smiled with warmth and understanding. "No, I'm not, but my friends at school were and my sister is. So, I've learned a thing or two over the years and I just don't want you to be uncomfortable, sweetheart. I know you don't know these men well yet but trust me please. These three boys are good men, and with a true scent match, well sometimes you have to break the rules and step out of your comfort zone to find where you truly belong."

I nibbled on my inner lip, my pulse quickening. I didn't want to move in with them immediately. I'd never done it before and wasn't sure I even could.

Susie walked over to me, sat down on the bed, and reached out for my hand.

I immediately inched closer to her, craving the closeness that came with a mother/daughter relationship. Thanks to the jerk Alphas in the pack I came from, it was yet another thing I never truly had. We weren't allowed that closeness. We'd only ever been tools to be used. I shivered as the memories washed over me.

"Sweetheart, why don't you want to go back to their house and nest there? I promise you'll be much more comfortable there."

I didn't want to answer her, at least not at length. I barely knew these guys or her. We'd only just met, and I wasn't sure I could just spill the proverbial beans. My walls might have come down, but I was still wary, which was only natural, all things considered.

She turned around and flicked her hand at the three towering men as if they were errant children lingering around their mother's skirts. "Go on. You lot find something to do in the office for half an hour. The girls need to talk."

I didn't want them to go, and from the way they all looked at me with yearning in their eyes, they didn't want to leave either. But one by one, they obeyed Susie's command, and all three men left my motel room, giving us some semblance of privacy.

I stared after them, then turned to meet her gaze, gob smacked. "How did you do that?" I asked, my brows furrowed and my mouth ajar.

She simply grinned at me. "You mean, how did I get three Alphas to do as I asked?"

I nodded my head, still reeling. The type of Alphas I'd met in the past would never have listened to a woman. Women were beneath men—always—especially Alphas. It was the sort of unspoken pack rule one just learned and was forced to accept as a part of life. We had our place, and they had theirs.

She smiled gently at me. "They respect me. They always have. All three are good men," she reiterated. "They're a rare combination of Alphas, and you're one lucky woman."

I nodded before I realized I was doing it. She was right. I was lucky, although I wasn't particularly feeling it. There was a tightness in my chest that refused to go away, and I knew without question that it was because my men weren't with me. It felt like a part of me was being yanked out of my body, as if my heart were on a string, and they'd walked away with it.

You're being dramatic. Just stop it.

"Look," Susie said, gripping my hand a little harder. "I know you don't know me, and I don't know you. But I know these men, hon, all of them, since they were babies. And they would never hurt you. So, if you're worried about trusting them…"

"Oh, I know they wouldn't hurt me," I said honestly, knowing it somewhere deep in my bones. "But I can't lose my freedom just as soon as I've found it. My mom… she said—" I swallowed hard, cutting myself off before I gave this relative stranger my whole life story.

Stranger or the mother of one of my mates?

Susie sighed in silent understanding. "Look, I'll make you a deal. You can have this motel room for as long as you like. I'll take it off the books, okay? It's all yours, rent free. It'll be a safe space if you feel you ever need it, A place to get away."

"Oh, I couldn't impose," I began.

"You're not," Susie assured me sternly. "Besides, I only run this place. It's Michael who owns it. And if you're his true scent match, then he'll want you to have whatever you want. So, while it's my suggestion, sweetheart, ultimately the offer is to help make you feel comfortable and secure, which benefits your whole pack."

I wrapped my arms around myself as unbidden tears filled my eyes. I'd never known such generosity or luxury. I'd never before been given a free meal, let alone been offered permanent lodging, a safe haven for my anxious and world-weary soul.

"All that being said," Michael's mother continued, "you've got to set up your nest in their house—your home. They have spare bedrooms and extra space for your things. Just *please* trust me on this. You won't feel safe with your nest here. We get busy at all times of year, and people can get really loud over the holidays. And if I've learned anything from my omega friends over the years, is the desire to feel safe and secure overrides all else."

I inhaled deeply, trying to center myself and absorb her words.

What she was saying made sense. I'd never wanted to mate with anyone in my life, nor had I felt the primal urge to nest before. It felt confusing and strange. But there was a light in the darkness of my confusion, and that was the fact that I'd finally done what my mother begged me to.

I've found my true scent matches.

"Okay, Susie," I agreed. "I'll go with them, but I'm not staying in their bedrooms. I'd like my own space."

Susie smiled kindly and stood up, pulling me along with her. "I'd recommend the loft. It's big and light. Now, let's get you packed up so the boys can take you home to eat and rest." Without another word, Susie started packing up all my things.

I sank back down onto the mattress, giving myself time to take in everything that had happened to me. I'd only meant to drive through this town and not look back. It was supposed to be nothing more than a pit stop on the road to my future.

And yet look what fate has brought me... three unique and gorgeous Alpha mates!

All I had to do was hope and pray that they would treat me better than my fathers had ever treated my mother. After all, what was the point of having your perfect mates if all they wanted was a slave to fulfill their every desire?

Surely, my men want more than that.

If that weren't true, they definitely would have been mated already. Handsome men didn't deny themselves if they could get what they wanted.

They've been waiting for a reason—for me.

Suppressing my anxiety, I sighed and got back to my feet to fetch and pack up my toiletries I'd stored in the bathroom earlier. Fate had reached out a helping hand and stranded me in that snowstorm. I was sure of it and wasn't about to look a gift horse in the mouth.

I've found my destiny at long last.

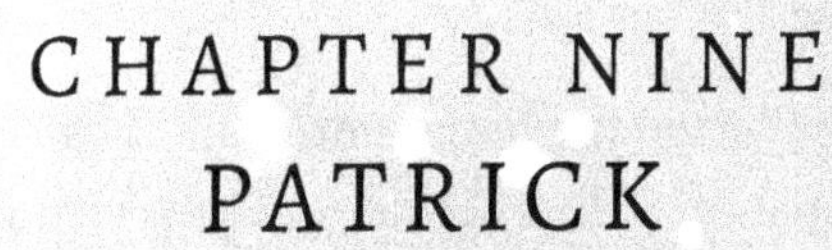

CHAPTER NINE
PATRICK

My body hummed with natural recognition and a warm sense of happiness that I only ever felt when Matilda was around. I couldn't have stopped the rush of adrenaline her presence inspired in me if I tried, nor did I want to. I'd never felt more alive. "So, this is the house," I said awkwardly as we stood right in front of the big white thing.

Matilda's breath hitched in her throat as she stared up at the double-story monstrosity with a picturesque wraparound porch. "It's beautiful," she whispered, a genuine look of awe on her face.

I couldn't help but smile as I scratched the back of my neck. "Thanks. Yeah, well… I bought it a long time ago. But when the three of us formed a pack, we renovated it together, added the porch and more. Let me show you inside." I put a hand against the small of Matilda's back and led her to the front door. David and Michael were right behind us, and I could practically *feel* their impatience vibrating through their every breath.

I unlocked the front door and pushed it open to reveal a grand entrance, complete with a spiral staircase. I'd thought it was a ridiculous extravagance back in the day, but now, looking at the sheer wonder and happiness written all over Matilda's face as she looked upon her new home? It made everything we'd endured, everything we'd done, and everything we'd waited for, worthwhile.

"Come up to the loft first," David said brightly, taking her by the hand and tugging her toward the stairs. "I think you'll like that space the best."

"Maybe she should see the basement first?" I called after them. "So that she has a comparison." But neither of them responded to my idea.

In fact, Matilda actually giggled in delight as she and David raced up the stairs like teenagers escaping their parents.

I grimaced. I didn't appreciate that David had just stepped in and seemed to be rushing her. Of the three of us, I was aware that he'd spent the least time with our mate, but from what I'd garnered, that wasn't the right way to go about things with her, especially as she was still clinging to the concept of her freedom so desperately. She wasn't ready to go all in, and I understood that, so why didn't he?

A better plan would have been to give her a full tour of the house first, so that she could weigh her options and acclimatize to her unfamiliar environment. Pushing her straight into what was essentially the attic, as airy and light as it was, didn't feel like the logical move.

What if she thinks we're trying to hide her?

"Maybe we should show her the spare room too?" I called up the stairs after them, then snorted with mild annoyance.

Wouldn't she need a bedroom as well as the loft space? And shouldn't she see the basement as well, just in case? She might like the warmth and darkness of the basement. It would be kind of like being in cave, safe, tucked away, an unexposed.

Where is the best place for her nest?

In truth, I didn't know. I was only guessing and just going off what information I'd picked up over the years. But I hadn't had a mate before, let alone an actual omega. They seemed to have their own set of rules if my memory served.

Michael shut the front door behind us and locked it with a definite *click*.

I glanced back at him and nodded once. We understood each other, Michael and me. While David could be a right royal pain in the ass with his sunshiny attitude toward everything, Michael was much more grounded.

Michael inclined his head, tipping it in the direction of staircase, a subtle suggestion. "Shall we go see what changes she wants to make to the loft?" he asked.

I grunted in agreement. He was probably right. We were, after all, in a hurricane of all things *new*, so we might as well step into the eye of the storm and not worry about the order of things. I joined Michael in climbing the stairs to the second floor where most of the bedrooms were, and then we walked over to the small staircase that led us up to the loft.

We started climbing the ladder, and as my head cleared floor level, I looked around the light-filled room. We didn't really use the loft except for storage, and it was a space that I'd argued against renovating at the time. I'd thought it was a stupid and unnecessary extra expense. But Michael and David had pushed for it and now…

"Oh my! It's the most perfect space ever!" Matilda declared.

I shook my head as a smile stretched my lips. Now our mate was squealing with delight, spinning like a pinwheel as she drank in the room. It was one of the most memorable moments of my life, just witnessing her euphoria. I sniffed the air, sneezing loudly as my sinuses were assaulted. "It could use a dusting," I suggested.

"And some new furniture," David said, running his hand over the old sofa in the middle of the room. It was the same one I'd had in my twenties, which had definitely seen better days. The whole room was a cluttered mess for the time being. We'd stored everything we didn't want in the house up here, which meant there were boxes of every size, filing cabinets, extra pillows, rugs, and chests of drawers.

"No!" Matilda cried aloud, throwing herself dramatically onto the old brown leather sofa with beer stains and a tear or two. She clung to it like she'd never let it go. "This is perfect. I'll get to cleaning right away." A heartbeat later, she jumped up and threw her jacket off, revealing the slender frame I'd gotten *very* well acquainted with in my truck not so long ago.

Suddenly, my pants were feeling too hot and much too tight for my liking. I cleared my throat. "I'll... um... go get the cleaning supplies." With that, I excused myself before my body had the chance to take over, and I jumped our mate again.

David and Michael would not appreciate that.

Despite having a cleaner who visited once a week, she didn't do the loft. There had never been any point. Even so, I knew where she kept everything we needed—the utility closet.

By the time I got back upstairs, the room looked totally different. I'd half expected to walk back into the room and find the guys naked and on top of Matilda. I wouldn't have blamed them, honestly. I'd already had my turn to mate with her, so to speak, and they were no doubt hanging out to claim their mate too. But instead, they were studiously moving furniture around. They were maneuvering it all to the center of the room, pushing it together to create one huge bed of a sort.

I couldn't help but chuckle as I put the bucket down and began pulling out cleaning supplies. Susie was right. Matilda's omega instincts were kicking in and driving her to build a nest made from our combined pieces of old furniture. Our scents would be all over the leather and aged materials. I sprayed some disinfectant on the coffee table nearest to me and wiped the cloth over the thick layer of dust.

Matilda jumped at me with an unexpected screech, her eyes wide and panicked. "No! Please, let me do it!" she pleaded.

I frowned at her. "Ah, I do know how to clean, Matilda. We don't expect you to be our housekeeper."

She took the spray bottle and the cloth from me before I could touch anything else and clutched the bottle and rag tightly to her chest. She was staring at me with wariness and concern in her eyes. It appeared as if she was worried that I might react badly to her request. Like I might hurt her.

The very thought unnerved me, rattling me to my core. That was learned behavior. She was being defensive, readying herself for a possible confrontation.

What has she lived through?

"I know," she said quickly, though there was no way she could actually have known how I felt about the house and gender roles. "But I don't want you wiping the smells off everything. I can't explain it, I'm sorry. Please don't be mad."

I stood back and began to laugh, though the trouble in her eyes gave me pause. Her request was innocent enough, and I wasn't about to argue with our new mate. "No, no," I said. "I understand. It's an omega thing, and I wouldn't know what smells you wanted versus the ones you don't."

Though dusting and vacuuming couldn't hurt, surely?

She bit her lower lip, worrying it between her teeth, and leaned forward as though drawn by a magnet. Then she perfumed, her scent blossoming around her like a cloud of tangible lust.

While I could resist before, there was no stopping my primal side a moment longer. I reached out and wrapped a possessive hand around her tiny waist, pulling her against my body. "Come here, baby girl," I crooned, unable to prevent the raw force of our attraction tearing through me.

She whimpered in the sexiest way, her hands coming up to press against my chest as her knees gave way and she slumped against me.

I groaned deep in my throat. "Damn it, Matilda, I can't keep my hands off you when you look at me like that."

"I can't help it," she whispered, tilting her head up so she was speaking against my lips. "You smell so good—you *all* do—especially in here."

My gaze flicked up to my packmates' faces. It was abundantly clear they were just as affected as I was by her scent, especially now that it was in full force. I dropped my head to kiss her lips gently, then turned her around to face David and Michael. I was as hard as a rock and took immense pleasure in pressing my cock against her ass. Hearing her answering gasp of approval when she felt me set my insides ablaze.

But this time is for them. I've already been to heaven.

I leaned down to whisper into her ear, my breath hot against her flesh. "I think your other mates would like a taste of you. What do you think, baby?"

She moaned softly, bumping her ass back against my groin once more in invitation.

"Go on, sweetheart," I urged and gave her a little push toward them before I took what she was offering and bent her over the old couch.

Matilda stumbled toward David first. "I'm sorry I left this morning. I shouldn't have run away like that..." She trailed off.

"It's okay," he said, reaching out to steady her. "I know you felt the link too, didn't you?"

She nodded silently as she stepped willingly into his arms, the relief in her demeanor evident.

With a satisfied and gentle smile, David reached around her and held her tightly while her arms wrapped around his neck. A breathless fragment of time stretched between them, then they kissed.

I felt a jab of irrational jealousy inside that was hard to squash. Swallowing hard, I looked away, spying an old rocking chair in the corner and making my way over to it.

She's not just my mate... she's our *mate.*

I was part of a pack, which meant that I had to be fine with sharing Matilda with David and Michael. It was something I'd always known when we naturally formed our unlikely group of Alphas all those years ago, but even so, for a brief moment, it seemed harder to process than I'd expected.

Her moan had me looking up and watching, even though I didn't mean to. Once my gaze found her, I couldn't turn away. My cock throbbed and ached as Tilly's clothes fell away piece by piece.

She moaned again and gasped, her head falling back in ecstasy as David kissed her neck, and Michael stripped off nearby.

I was definitely *still* jealous. My fingers curled into fists, and there was a deep, dark, weight lingering in my belly.

What are you doing?

I mentally chastised myself. We'd waited so long for her, I wasn't going to be the one to fuck it all up. Besides, she was *so* incredibly hot and after this, when we'd all had the chance to bond with her, she would be ours to share forever.

Her moaning and groaning penetrated my brain like music to my ears, and my eyes fell upon her erect nipples with laser focus, my cock twitching in my pants.

Wow... I could definitely get used to this.

If I could overcome my stubborn insecurities for anyone, it was her.

CHAPTER TEN
TILLY

*D*avid's lips were so soft, their touch sent shivers of delight fizzling up my spine, and his hands were *everywhere*. My heat flared inside me, hungry like a ravenous fire, and it needed more fuel. *I* needed more. I hurriedly pushed at my clothes, desperately wanting to be naked, to feel his hands on my burning skin.

David moaned and dropped his head, pressing his lips to my neck.

I tilted my head to the side and slid my fingers through his hair, reveling in the way he felt against me. His scent reminded me of Michael's, but with a little more cinnamon and spice. He smelled like a delicious apple-cinnamon oatmeal crumble. Soft, wickedly sweet, and crisp, all at once. I gasped aloud as his lips captured my nipple and he sucked it into his mouth as his hand slid between my thighs. "Oh, fuck," I moaned and kicked my jeans away.

Michael moved up behind me then and turned my face to him with his fingers.

Damn, he's stunning.

Those eyes would make any child of his the envy of every mother around.

He kissed me hard and fast, stealing my breath away as I was briefly sandwiched between them.

"Let's lay her down," I heard David say, though it sounded far away. "I want to taste her pussy."

My blood pounded in my ears, and I couldn't hear properly above the sound of my own racing heart. Before I could even register what was happening, I felt myself moved onto the pile of pillows in the center of the room. Patrick's scent hit me in waves, combining with the rest of the pack's, to create a medley of delicious and mouthwatering aromas.

I cried out with unabashed pleasure as they descended on me. But as Michael and David ravished me, I yearned for Patrick too. I wanted them all.

Where is he?

But a moment later, David's lips found the inside of my thigh, and I stopped thinking altogether. "Oh…" No one had ever gone down on me before, and I wasn't sure how to respond. Trusting in my heat and instincts, pleasure unlike anything I'd ever felt roared to life between my thighs as David devoured my pussy.

He greedily lapped at my juices, his tongue flicking my clit with pinpoint precision. On and on, he dined upon me as if I were a Michelin star meal, triggering every nerve and pleasure center in my body.

"Oh… fuuuckkkk…" My belly tightened as I spasmed up to grab at him.

Michael lay down beside me, stroking my nipples and kissing my lips. He was being sweet and sensual, but it was all going too slowly.

I'm going to explode!

"Come up," I gasped out at him. "Please, Michael. I want you in my mouth."

His eyes widened for a second in what seemed to be a *this it too good to be true* kind of look before he was kneeling beside my head and lowering himself down for me.

"Yes…" I breathed, hungry to taste him for the first time. His cock was lovely and long and had a large, bulbous head. I couldn't think straight, but the fleeting mental image of him being inside me had me moaning in anticipation. I grabbed the shaft with my hand, relishing in the warmth of his flesh in my palm. Unable to wait a second longer, I wrapped my lips around his head.

Michael groaned loudly, his breath hitching in his throat in the sexiest way imaginable.

Then David slid his fingers into me, slowly pumping, exploring and teasing, his touch like fire blazing inside me.

Fuck... I need more.

I pulled my lips from Michael's cock and glanced down at David, making brief eye contact. "Please. More. *You.*" I sounded incoherent, even to my own ears, but I didn't care. My face felt like it was probably bright red, and my pussy literally pulsed with my heat. I needed all of them everywhere. Now.

David didn't need to be told twice and jumped up at my desperate invitation. He shoved some pillows under my ass, bringing me up to him so he could stand between my thighs.

"Oh, yes… please…" I begged.

Like a true, sexy gentleman, Michael pulled away momentarily, deferring to the pack member between my legs.

David wasted no time. He grabbed my thighs and pushed them apart, his gaze full of lust and something deeper, something infinitely more heart-stopping.

I reached for him, my heart leaping in my chest as I grabbed his forearms to anchor myself in the storm of my heat.

He rubbed his cock over my pussy. "You want this?" he asked, drawing out my delicious anguish. "Tell me you want me."

I thrust my hips toward him, needing him inside me more than it felt like my lungs needed air. "I want you!" I practically screamed. "Fuck me. Please!"

An almost inhuman growl rolled through him, and he thrust his thick cock into my needy pussy.

Pleasure exploded inside me, fireworks of rainbow light erupting behind my eyelids as I came instantly.

"Fuck," David hissed, grabbing my thighs with urgency as I groaned, shuddered, and cried out around him. Then he stilled within me, simply filling me up with his huge, pretty cock, enduring the chaos of my ecstasy with a strength of will I'd never seen before.

My eyes rolled back in my head, and I clung to him, my anchor in the storm of the first heat I hadn't suppressed. I gasped for air as I began to come down from my pinnacle, light-headed and breathless.

David's gaze bore into my own and he began to move, withdrawing to his tip, then sliding back inside me, every thrust lighting my insides on fire.

It was like nothing I'd ever experienced. I made noises I'd never made before, and the pleasure just kept coming. And when David sped up, chasing his own bliss and fucking me hard and deep, I came again and *again*, until every inch of me felt like a live wire, over-sensitive, and slick with desire.

When David couldn't hold on any longer, he spilled his hot seed inside me in a torrent of sticky delirium. His deep-throated groan sounded so incredibly fucking hot, and with every pulse of heat inside of me, my pussy rippled around him. And when he collapsed on top of me, there were tears in my eyes.

I'd never known sex could feel like this. If I had known, I would never have stayed with *any* of those other packs, hoping in vain for some sense of connection and belonging. One kiss from any of my three men has told me what I needed to know.

Leaning up, I kissed his sweaty neck and clung to his back, which was hot and clammy.

So hot... My God, he is hot.

David lifted his head, an almost dopey, sweet smile on his face. "You are incredible."

I laughed, unable to contain myself. "Um... no. That was all you."

He kissed me gently in response, then pulled away. "I don't think so, baby."

All things considered, I should have been totally satisfied, but instead, when I came to my senses and saw Michael lying nearby—still hard and waiting—my desire swirled to life once more, an insatiable beast with a mind of its own.

All the while Patrick was sitting, still fully clothed, simply watching, his gaze intense and dark. I wasn't sure if he would want me after the other two had fucked me. I hoped so, but at this moment, I didn't care. I needed to be claimed by the whole pack—that's all that mattered—and Patrick had already staked his claim. Trusting my instincts, I sat up and got to my feet, then walked the two steps over to Michael.

"Hello, beautiful," he said, sliding his legs off the couch before pulling me into his lap.

"Michael," I breathed as I straddled him with ease and rubbed my aching pussy along his hard cock.

"Are you sure you can handle me too? I don't want to hurt you."

I nodded, lifting up so I could feel him beneath me. Then I reached down and put him exactly where I needed him. "You won't. I promise."

"All right, baby," Michael crooned as he grabbed my hips and pulled me down on him, impaling my pussy on his glorious cock.

I began to ride him, sparks of pleasure immediately sparking inside my brain.

This is crazy. I'm totally insatiable!

I bounced on his cock, reveling in the feel of his length until he flipped us over, lifted my legs up in the air, and slammed into me again and again. He pumped into my hungry pussy like a marathon runner—steady, constant, and unrelenting—until we were both crying out with our simultaneous orgasms. We collapsed against the pillows in a flurry of sweat, and my eyes fluttered shut. Michael was tall and lean, and *so* athletic. It was going to be so much fun trying to keep up with him, I could already tell.

Patrick!

My eyes snapped open and I sat up. "Patrick?"

My gorgeous sheriff Daddy stood up and sauntered over. "Yes, baby girl?" he purred.

"Will you join us?" I asked, my plaintive gaze seeking his.

He nodded and began to strip off, his hard cock bouncing up to hit his abdomen when he freed himself from his pants. The head was weeping with pre-cum and was even more perfect than I remembered it being in the truck.

I got up from my impromptu and chaotic nest, rising to my feet once more.

He frowned. "I was going to lie down with you," he said.

I kissed him, then whispered, "In a minute, maybe? I need to catch my breath, but I need you close."

He chuckled gently. "It's okay, baby. You've got this. You can handle one more."

I nodded, eyes wide as my chest heaved. "I can." I was starting to feel fatigued, but there was no way I was going to turn down the chance to be fucked by the sheriff again.

He turned me around and placed a hand on my back, bending me over the couch at my waist. "Hold onto the edge of the couch," he instructed.

I complied without shame, obeying the deep sense of need in my soul. My skin felt clammy, and my long blonde hair was a mess that fell over my shoulders and back in damp, sweaty, sexy waves.

Patrick spread my legs with his knees in a deliciously Alpha move, lined up his cock, and buried himself hilt-deep into me again. I was already wet beyond measure and more than just a little bit tender, but Patrick took his time, dealing me long, smooth strokes, and wringing one final, soul-shattering orgasm out of me. Together, we toppled over the edge.

Utterly spent, the pack's desire oozing from between my thighs, I crawled into my thrown together nest and burst into tears. Because when you find heaven on earth, surely that's the only *real* way to respond.

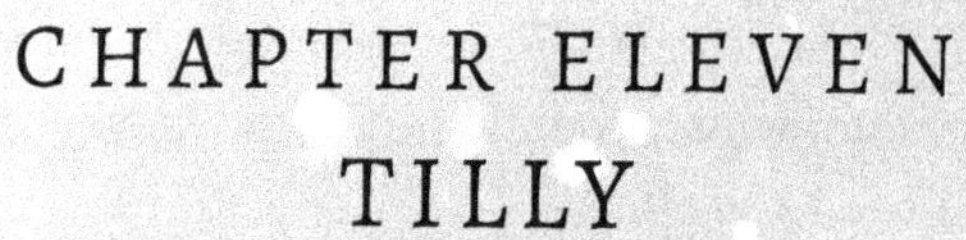

CHAPTER ELEVEN
TILLY

My amazing men held me as I cried, which seemed kind of ridiculous, but it was *exactly* what I needed—to let out all my stress and worries while wrapped up in their adoration and care. I couldn't believe I'd finally found them. The pack I'd dreamed of. The true scent matches my mother hoped I'd find.

After several minutes, Michael gently eased himself away to fetch some tissues for me, while David got me a cold glass of water, all while Patrick held me tight.

My perfect pack.

When I'd finally come down from my emotional high, and was relaxed enough to close my eyes, I thanked whatever Heavenly being had prompted me to stop in this small town. Lying in my very own nest with my men was the most beautiful moment of my life to date. And the sex… *mind blowing* was barely adequate to describe what we'd just shared.

"Should we go out for dinner?" Michael asked gently, stroking my hair with his free hand as he passed me my water.

I glanced over at him, connecting with his soul-meltingly striking blue eyes. "Um…" I was going to say *No, I wasn't hungry and I never wanted to move again.* My bones had disappeared into oblivion completely after that round of soul-shattering orgasms, and I wanted to lie here forever, in a mess of delirium like a jellyfish.

But before I could, my stomach answered for me. Loudly. I laughed at my traitorous belly with amusement. Apparently, a session with my men had taken more out of me than I'd imagined. "I think I could eat," I said with a soft smile. "Can we maybe go to that diner in town? The one with the cool drive-through and the fifties décor?"

Michael grinned at me as if he'd won the lottery. "Yeah, of course. My sister happens to work there. We can say hello while we're there."

My eyebrows rose high on my forehead, and I peered up at my mate with curiosity.

What are the odds...

"Her name isn't Hollie, is it?"

It was Michael's turn to look surprised. "How'd you know that?" he asked, looking down on me with love.

I sighed and rested my head back against Patrick's chest. Fate was funny like that, it seemed. "I met her the first night I was here when I went there for something to eat. She's really awesome."

Michael's eyes lit up with familial affection and pride. "Yeah, she sure is," he agreed.

Patrick squeezed me gently. "Should we go?" he asked, his breath hot against my ear. "They close in an hour, so we had better get moving"

I groaned loudly and yawned as I struggled to sit up. I still felt like a bowl of wobbly Jello. "I want to stay here forever," I announced without thinking as I wiggled my fingers and toes, willing blood flow to return to my extremities. The silence that followed my declaration was deafening. It was so loud, in fact, that I glanced around at my pack in a panic, worried they'd suddenly disappeared because I'd said something terribly wrong.

David cleared his throat and offered me a warm smile "Well, you can."

"I can?" I repeated, not exactly sure what he meant.

I can... what?

He nodded. "Yeah, you can stay here forever. If you want."

Now, I was embarrassed. I'd meant it more in the way that as someone who'd slept rough her whole life, constantly teetering on the edge of fear and loneliness, living in a pile of pillows with three gorgeous men felt like heaven by comparison. "Well, how about dinner first?" I asked, grinning at him to avoid addressing the seriousness of the topic. I knew these three amazing men were my pack. But I had *so* many mental blocks and personal insecurities to overcome before I committed to staying and living with them forever. I needed a little time to adjust. I could literally feel them inside my mind, and I didn't even know what to do with that. It was as incredible as it was a tiny bit frightening.

"Dinner it is, then!" Patrick announced, sitting up and sliding out of my nest. One by one, the men got up and pulled their clothes back on.

I sighed. It was such a waste for them to have to get dressed again. All of them were handsome in a different and unique way that I appreciated. Patrick was burly with thick muscles, and looked just like a mountain man should, while Michael and David were lighter and leaner. But my God, they were just as luscious with their long, strong muscles and the tightest asses possible.

Michael glanced at me and winked as he buttoned up his shirt. "Are you coming, babe? Or shall we bring you something back?"

I'm not being left behind!

A small surge of panic at the mere thought of being apart from them, even for a brief time, got me moving. "I'm coming!" I said as I scrambled out of bed and reached for my clothes. I really needed to get my other jeans and do some laundry.

My guys dressed so well, I probably needed to go shopping and buy some new stuff too. I didn't want to look like some sort of raggamuffin they'd pulled off the street, even if I kind of was.

Once dressed, David grabbed my hand and led me downstairs and outside. There were three near-new trucks and cars parked outside that I hadn't noticed on our way in.

"Should we take the Lexus?" David asked. "It's the most comfortable," he reasoned.

Patrick snorted, a good-humored chuckle escaping his throat. "She didn't mind the truck this afternoon."

Mortification struck me, and my cheeks flared with heat and color. "Daddy!" I squealed, reaching over and whacking the sheriff playfully in the chest with my palm.

The guys all shared furtive glances as Patrick literally puffed up his chest and repeated back to me, "Um… Daddy?"

Oh, fuck.

"Did I just say that out loud?" I asked sheepishly, unable to tear the hysterical grin from my face. I felt like a little kid who'd been caught with her hand in the cookie jar.

Michael chuckled. "Oh, yeah. You did," he confirmed with amusement.

I inhaled sharply, and my free hand strayed to toy with my hair. "Um… well. It kind of suits you and it's—"

"Kinky, maybe? A little bit dirty?" Patrick asked, a wicked grin curving his lips.

"Ah…" I could only nod, unable to speak now that I was blushing fiercely. Every inch of me felt like it was on fire, and my face hurt from grinning so much.

"Come here, baby girl." Patrick pulled me into his arms and kissed me so thoroughly and deeply that my head was literally spinning with stars when he finally let me come up for air.

Michael pulled me back into his arms, pressing his arousal into my lower back. "You two had better stop that, or we aren't going to be getting to dinner any time soon."

That's not such a bad idea…

David laughed at my expression and took the lead, swinging his keys around his finger before he opened the vehicle with a press of his thumb. "Let's go."

The guys hustled me into the car, and with slow kisses all the way there, we made our way the two minutes to the diner. As we got out of the vehicle, the guys moved around me like a true pack. One of them was always holding my hand, the others playing offense and defense, ready for anyone who might dare to approach.

Michael's sister, Hollie, hurried over, a blur of smiles and bright blue hair.

"Oh my God. Michael! Is this your—" She gasped, her eyes wide.

"Hollie, this is Matilda. She's our mate. We finally found her."

Hollie flicked David away with a flippant gesture and grabbed both of my hands in hers. "Wow. You're from the other night! I knew there was something special about you," she said excitedly. "I felt it. Here." She let go of one of my hands and guided it to her chest so that I could feel her beating heart.

Hot tears welled up in my eyes at the simple truth that Hollie would be the first sister I ever had. A woman I could trust. "Me too," I admitted, touched.

She pulled me into her arms and hugged me so tightly, I could barely breathe—and I didn't care. "I'm so happy for you," she whispered into my ear. "My brother's the best. But don't tell him I said that."

I choked out a laugh as I pulled back gently and wiped at the tears in my eyes. "I won't."

The guys corralled me into a booth at the back of the restaurant.

Hollie followed, grabbing her pen and pad. "So, you guys know the menu," she prompted. "What do you want?"

The men shot out their orders in rapid succession. Burgers, fries, onion rings, shakes, and soda. It all sounded so good.

Hollie looked at me with a grin. "And will you be wanting your burger and pie again?"

I nodded, leaning into Michael, who was sitting beside me, his possessive hand gripping my thigh. "Thanks, Hollie."

My new sister hurried away with a sigh and a contented smile. It was abundantly clear that she was genuinely happy for her brother and his pack, and it was heartwarming to see.

A real family.

"I'd like to work at a place like this," I said, looking around at the clean diner appreciatively. "Do you think they're hiring?"

The guys froze and did that weird thing they did when they looked at each other and didn't speak, but they were communicating.

"What is it?" I demanded, sounding more annoyed than I'd meant to.

Michael cleared his throat. "Um… you really don't need to work, beautiful. We make more than enough money between the three of us, and the house is already paid off." Before he dug his proverbial grave any deeper, he stopped talking, which showed that he had more brains than all my exes put together. He read the warning on my face.

Good job.

I turned to look across the booth and addressed the three of them all at once. "Look, I need to make something clear. I met you all *yesterday*. I'm *not* looking for a pack to take care of me, financially especially. I'm not saying that you would do this, but I grew up with a mother who was literally at the mercy of my fathers. She had no money, no friends, and no choices. The only way I've survived the last five years without my family or support is because I've worked my ass off, always made sure I've had my own money and paid my way." I was practically panting with the emotional toll of dredging up the past, but I got it all out in the end.

Didn't they realize that sacrificing my right to a job was sacrificing my safety and my ability to leave if I needed to. I wouldn't do that.

The guys glanced at each other for another moment, then Patrick spoke, seemingly the Alpha of the Alphas. "The owner, Danny, is a friend of ours. If you want an interview, I'm sure he'd be happy to set one up with you."

It was my turn to glance from one man to the next, unable to stand the awkward silence.

Is that all they have to say?

"That's it?" I asked, waiting for the inevitable battle that I fought against every pack I dated.

Patrick frowned. "Yeah, baby girl. What else is there?"

Hollie arrived at the booth with our drinks and paused once she'd handed them out. "Everything okay here?" she asked, one brow quirked.

Patrick wasted no time. "Hey, Hollie. Can you tell Danny that Matilda is interested in working here and would like an interview?"

Hollie shrugged casually, tucking a stray lock of blue hair behind her ear. "Yeah, sure, no problem. Do you have a cell number I can pass along?"

I nodded as she pushed her pen and pad over the smooth laminate table to me. "Um, yeah… thanks," I said. "And Tilly's fine, by the way." I quickly scribbled my details down and slid the pen and paper back.

Where am I? The twilight zone?

Why wasn't Hollie telling me I didn't need to work—that her brother would take care of me? And why weren't my guys fighting tooth and nail to keep me dependent on them? It's what all the Alphas from my past had done.

But I'd never let them get control over me. Not again. It was only when I'd run, when my mother sent me on my way with nothing but a bit of cash, a coat, and her love, that I'd discovered what freedom could feel like.

Hollie picked her pad and pen back up. "Cool," she said. "I'll be back with your orders soon."

I slumped into my seat, leaning heavily on Michael. "You know… I was kind of expecting more push back than that."

David chuckled, but it was full of warmth and there was no trace of mockery or cruelty in his voice when he spoke. "Yeah, that much was obvious, gorgeous."

Patrick drummed his fingers on the table as he met my gaze. "We're not your keepers, baby girl. We thought you wouldn't want to work, but if you want to, go for it. We all do and we'll support you no matter what."

I would have cried if I hadn't felt so relieved. "Thank you," I said with a repressed sniffle. "That means a lot to me. Thanks for understanding."

Our food arrived soon after, and we ate way too fast, the rich aromas of everything making my mouth literally water. I passed the time between mouthfuls by asking the guys questions about their jobs and quickly worked out that I would be lucky to see all three of them at home at once. They all worked different shifts, and if I also worked, it would make quality time together really difficult.

That truth wouldn't stop me from applying for a job, of course. I couldn't lose my independence. It was the only thing that kept me safe, even now.

"Do you think I can take the apple pie to go?" I asked, staring down at the scrumptious looking dessert. "I can't eat it all now." In fact, I couldn't even take another single bite. My poor stomach was already stretched to the maximum.

"Yeah, of course. I'll be right back." Michael picked up the plate, stood, and walked over to where Hollie was busy balancing the register for the night.

Patrick slid off his seat and held out his hand to me. "Time to go home, baby?"

I glanced at his hand then looked up at his face.

Oh, yeah... I'd follow him anywhere.

I nodded, not trusting myself to say anything else. These men had a huge home, and a part of me was afraid that far too easily, their house was going to become my home.

Am I ready for this?

I FOUND MY SEA ROUTE
HALIFAX

CHAPTER TWELVE
DAVID

Sunshine streamed into the room and warmed my face, searing my eyes beneath my lashes. I groaned and blinked rapidly, not impressed with myself. Had I forgotten to draw the curtains last night? There was no way I was going back to sleep with such bright light.

Why would I have left the... Oh.

My moving hands found a warm leg, and my heart skipped a beat. Memories of the night before flooded back to me, and a wave of pleasure and peace swept over my very bones.

My mate.

I turned my head slowly toward Tilly, her magnificent body still wrapped in comfortable blankets amidst the chaos of her nest.

God, she's stunning.

Her glorious, long blonde hair spread out over the pillows, and Patrick, who'd managed to get Tilly to fall asleep on him, was snoring soundly beneath her. As I admired our mate's beauty, nature called, so I slid out of the large non-bed to go to the nearby adjoining bathroom.

Last night had been nothing short of amazing. For that matter, all of yesterday was amazing. After the most incredible sex of my life, we'd gone out to dinner at the local diner and talked and laughed until well after closing time. When we'd returned home, Tilly had gone straight back to her nest and fallen asleep within moments.

She was far too thin and seemed exhausted by the weight of whatever stress she was carrying with her from the past. Her speech over dinner had spoken of deep-seated trust issues and an abusive family life that I couldn't even begin to fathom. My parents were both betas, so it had come as quite a surprise to the family when I'd shown natural Alpha traits. Though I'd been fortunate enough to have grown up with a sibling and parents who loved and respected one another. Growing up like she so obviously had wasn't something I'd wish on an enemy, let alone the beautiful, courageous woman that would grow to be my mate.

When I finally stepped back into the main area of the light-filled loft, the rest of my pack were all still asleep, resting peacefully in what would soon become our marriage bed. I stretched my arms over my head and tilted my neck back, my lower back cracking loudly like it did at the chiropractor office.

I'll order a super king mattress online today and hopefully it will fit over the top of those old couches. I can't keep sleeping on half a twenty-year-old sofa. I'm way too old for this.

Sneaking down the stairs, I went straight to the kitchen. I'd make them all breakfast, then head to work.

Work...

What was that niggling reminder sensation going off in my head? It was something important, I knew it.

Her heat suppressors! Crap.

I'd have to ask her whether she'd taken any since she picked them up yesterday. It didn't seem like it. Her response to us had been incredibly strong and visceral, but I couldn't discount the possibility that she'd taken one. If she had, it would unfortunately wreak havoc with her hormones for the day.

With a fridge that was always full of food, I got to work on a more decadent breakfast—that wasn't as protein-focused—than usual. I ignored the bacon, sausages, and eggs, instead, grabbing all the ingredients to make a mess of scrumptious crepes.

Once I'd made a large stack of thin, sweet crepes, I simmered up a fresh, sugary strawberry syrup and poured it all over the crepes that oozed over the sides in an aesthetically pleasing way, saturating the plate. I swirled an overly generous dollop of whipped cream on the top, then garnished it with a couple whole strawberries. My efforts looked like something that belonged on the cover of a country cooking magazine. I just hoped it made Tilly smile. If she enjoyed them, it'd be a boost to my ego, but seeing her smile would be worth it. The way she smiled with her eyes as much as her lips was hands-down, my favorite thing about her.

Damn, I can't wait to dig in!

Happy with the selection of treats, I grabbed the food, plates, and cutlery, then headed back to the loft. I wasn't very quiet as I approached the nest and regretted it only a touch when I saw our mate beginning to stir.

Tilly wriggled a little under the blankets and opened her eyes. She glanced around and physically jolted, looking confused and startled for a moment. Then her gaze settled on me and my crepes, her face immediately relaxing when she recognized me. "David," she said as a perfect smile lit up her face.

I smiled back, though my heart banged rapidly in my chest. I couldn't help but wonder if the intensity and overwhelming desire of our budding relationship would ever fade, and I found myself doubting that it would. It might dim to a comfortable, more stable glow that would endure the test of time, but it'd never stop feeling like I was with my mate—the woman who was perfect for me—and that would never not be my everything. "I made you breakfast, but I have to go."

"Oh, thank you!" she chirped as she began to carefully and slowly extricate herself from Patrick.

He grabbed her as though he'd slept beside her his whole life and stole a kiss before he let her free.

She reached for a fork as she crawled over, her tongue darting out to dampen her lips. "This looks amazing," she breathed. "Thank you so much, David."

Witnessing her heavenly smile and the look of genuine gratitude revealed in her vulnerable gaze, I couldn't help myself. I reached down and cupped her face, bringing her mouth to mine so I could taste her just once more before I left. Her lips melted into mine, and her soft moan shot straight to my groin no sooner than it met my ears. I groaned, pulling away reluctantly. Work was the last place I wanted to be, but responsibility and a strong sense of duty had been drilled into me from the day I was born. I couldn't bail on my staff or my customers. They were relying on me. "I have to go," I said again, placing the communal meal on the nearest flat surface by the nest—a short chest of drawers.

"Go?" Her eyes were wide and her pupils dilated. "Where?"

I would have laughed at her panicked response, except she was just *so* delicious and sweet that I couldn't. "Work," I said. "I have to open the pharmacy."

"Oh, right. Do you want me to get up?" she asked, moving as if she was going to slide out of bed.

"No. Stay," I said gently. "I need to shower and get dressed anyway, but I'll see you after work, okay?"

She nodded. "Okay."

I kissed her one more time, loving the desire that rose in her eyes as I stared down at her. Groaning, frustration ripped through me. I didn't have another pharmacist on the books at the moment, so I couldn't call in sick, even if I really needed to.

"Go," she whispered. "I'll be here when you get back. I promise."

Nodding, I still didn't like the feeling of having to leave her. "Okay, but make sure you choose a bedroom for yourself today so that you can have personal space if you need it."

She smiled, her cheeks delightfully rosy as she picked up the fork to start eating. "Thanks again for making breakfast, David. You're the best."

"Enjoy," I barely managed, tearing myself away and staggering with blue balls and a regretful heart to my own bathroom to get ready for work.

What are they going to do without me today? Does Patrick have to work? Does Michael?

For the first time, I wished I didn't own my own business and that there were several other pharmacists that could handle my shift for the day. I definitely wanted to spend a full day with our mate. I certainly deserved it, didn't I? Work was mockingly quiet, which made things even worse, and it was harder to bear the time away from our mate. It seemed like no one even needed me at the pharmacy.

I want to go home.

The hours felt like they were dragging by, but my day improved after my lunch break when Michael and Tilly walked into the pharmacy. Well, to be frank, she *ran* in, arms extended in open invitation.

"David!" she practically squealed as she ran up to my counter at the back of the store.

I couldn't help it, my whole body lit up with happiness at seeing her, and I stepped forward around the counter to meet her. I opened my arms as she excitedly launched herself at me, then buried my nose in her hair, inhaling her scent. My whole body relaxed as her familiar omega fragrance wafted over me.

Oh, God. Where have you been all my life?

"I missed you," Tilly whispered into my ear.

I lifted my head and pulled back, feeling my heart crack and break, only to be remade whole again in the blink of an eye. "I missed you, too," I admitted.

It was obvious to everyone in the house that Patrick had been lonely over the past few years. He'd been fucking grumpy as a result, but I hadn't thought I'd felt the same way. In fact, I would have bet good money I'd have been able to go another ten years without my mate and be fine. But now that I had her in my life and had claimed her, I wasn't so sure that would have actually been okay. I honestly couldn't imagine how I would have survived another single week without knowing how this surreal, scent-matched bonding felt.

Thank you to whatever Fates sent her my way.

"So, what are you guys doing here?" I asked, pulling away to stand behind my desk once more. I was at work and outside of a greeting embrace, I needed to be as professional as possible. Marie was already giving me the side-eye from across the store as she stocked shelves.

Michael threw his arm around Tilly and grinned. "We were just grabbing some lunch, but I have to head to work soon, and Patrick left hours ago."

Oh. So they haven't spent the entire day fucking without me. Good.

I glanced at the clock. "Well, I finish at four o'clock. Do you want to hang around here for a bit, Tilly? I'd be glad for the company."

She grinned but shook her head in apology. "I'd love to, but I was honestly just hoping to go home and have a little nap if that's okay. I'm kind of still exhausted..." She trailed off, worrying her lower lip between her teeth as her cheeks flared with color.

I couldn't hold in my laughter. "Of course. It's absolutely all right," I said. "Did you end up choosing a bedroom?"

She nodded and smiled at me. "Yeah, I'm just taking the spare one."

I snorted. I hadn't even thought about the fact that there was only one true spare bedroom in the house. "Oh, right... but you know any one of us would happily shift rooms if you want ours."

She shrugged like it was no big deal. "No, seriously. I like the spare room." Then she yawned and covered her mouth with her hand before rubbing her eyes.

I nodded at Michael, a subtle hint that he should take her home. "See you later on?" I prompted.

"See you," he said as he grinned and led her away.

A customer walked over to my counter as they left, and I switched straight back into work mode, a genuine smile on my face. But knowing my mate would be in my home, waiting for me when I got back there again, made the last few hours of my workday *infinitely* better.

CHAPTER THIRTEEN
MICHAEL

I cut my shift at the motel short and headed home around seven o'clock. My mom had everything under control—she always did—but the conversation we had mid-afternoon came as a surprise. She'd suggested we look into hiring additional staff so that I could spend more time at home with Tilly.

She didn't need to tell me twice!

Excitedly, I told her to start advertising and interviewing straight away, but then hesitated, catching myself before I got carried away. I wasn't sure about hiring anyone just yet. Based on our earlier conversations, it seemed like Tilly was hell-bent on working full-time as well, so I wasn't sure if hiring more staff would fix the problem. I didn't want to be sitting at home alone all week if she was going to be working all the time too.

As it was, all three of us worked *a lot*, which made sense for us while we were single. There really wasn't much else to do, so we'd poured our energies into building our careers and piling up cash for our future. David worked the most regular hours out of the three of us, but Patrick's shifts were all over the place, and I worked plenty of nights.

If Tilly wanted to do waitressing work alongside my sister, that would mean she could do any shift—nights, days, or weekends. I sighed, momentarily defeated. I didn't want to ask her to prioritize us over what she believed was her own financial security. We could offer her money so that she had her own nest egg to fall back on, but then she'd feel like we were paying her for sex, and that was the last thing any of us would want.

What is the solution here?

Tilly was our mate, and we were her true scent matches. Surely, we'd sort something out that worked for all of us? There just had to be a way. My sister's face popped into my head, and I smiled. Hollie had been wanting to help more at the motel. Maybe I could do less hours and teach her the managerial side of the motel business? I shook myself, not liking the creeping sense of dread that was slithering over my skin like a nest of unsettled snakes.

When I got home, David was sitting in the living room reading a book, and the whole house smelled of roast beef, garlic, and onion. "Smells good," I offered, inhaling deeply.

He lifted his hand and put his finger to his lips. "Shh… she's still sleeping," he warned.

I chuckled at how quickly he jumped to shush me. "So, is that how it's going to be from now on?" I asked. Our bachelor pad was already becoming a classic family home, with quiet rooms and dinner on the table by six. It was amazing how quickly life could change—practically in the blink of an eye.

David grinned, put his book down, and got up to join me in the kitchen. "While she's recovering from whatever it is she's recovering from… yeah. Definitely," he said.

I sighed, momentarily sobered by the allusion to Tilly's past. "Yeah… it seems like she has had a bad go of it before us."

He grabbed two beers out of the fridge and opened them. "Yeah, it certainly sounds like it. But never again," he answered.

I took the beer he offered and repeated the words like the oath that it was. "Never again," I agreed before taking a drink. A moment later, footsteps on the stairs had us both turning toward the sound. Tilly was rubbing her eyes and yawning like a sleepy little lamb, and I couldn't help the rush of love that swelled in my chest. "Hey, beautiful. How are you feeling?"

"I can't believe I slept so much," she groaned as she tugged at my hoodie that she'd stolen from my wardrobe, wrapping it around her further. Then she leaned against me, dropping her head on my shoulder. "How was your day?" she asked, sleep still thick in her voice.

I could barely speak. Was this how it felt to have a woman you loved? My head spun. How did mated men continue to work? How did they manage to leave their women at home? Already, I knew I was going to go crazy leaving her again tomorrow. "Oh… um, it was good, thank you. Mom was asking about you," I added.

She sighed and yawned again, obviously in need of even more sleep. "Your mother is so nice."

I didn't dare move, not wanting her to go anywhere as I gently placed an arm around her.

From the other side of the counter, David spoke gently to Tilly. "Do you ever see your mom at all?"

I almost groaned when she lifted her head and moved away from me.

No! Don't go!

But instead of being a five-year-old about it, I took her hand and pulled her toward the couch. "Come sit and tell us what's going on, baby girl." Pursing her lips and rubbing her eyes some more, she came with me and when I sat down, she moved straight into my lap like it was the most natural thing in the world. My arms slid around her and a sigh escaped me. It was impossible to keep it inside. Once upon a time, I would have considered myself a cool guy, but not anymore. Not when it came to my mate. Not when it came to our Matilda. "Tell us about your mom," I encouraged softly.

She tucked her head beneath my chin and nestled in. "She was a good mother, overall. But she… Well, I haven't seen her since the night she told me to run."

David cleared his throat from the other couch, and I tried hard not to flinch at the way she said, "told me to run."

Thankfully, David asked the question I couldn't voice. "That must be difficult for you, Tilly. But can you tell us what you mean when you say she told you to run? What did you have to run from?"

Or who?

Our mate sighed and slumped even further into herself.

I held her even tighter and crooned soothing nothings. "Sweetheart, if this is too painful, you don't have to tell us. We all have shit in our pasts that we'd rather not go into. We want to help, but we don't want to force you or make you feel uncomfortable."

Patrick more than us, but hey... we've all done things we'd rather not talk about.

She turned into me and inhaled deeply. Her eyes were closed, and slowly she relaxed against me, sitting up straighter. "No, it's not that. I can tell you, it's just not that interesting."

"It will be to us," I reassured her. "We want to know everything about you."

She sighed again but then started talking. "I grew up with three Alpha fathers, an omega mother, and three brothers. Once I hit puberty and my omega status was revealed, my brothers and fathers basically turned on me. Not that they treated me great before that, but being an omega was the bottom of the pile, according to them—the lowliest of the low."

I growled deep in my throat.

Fucking assholes.

"Go on," David said quietly. "Ignore Michael, he's just expressing how we both feel."

She blinked up at me, diverting her attention. "What do you mean?"

I gently gripped her chin and held her face still while I kissed her to settle myself down. Then I explained, "Omegas are not low. They should be at the top of the food chain. They're the mates we all want, the ones we actually need. Why should you be punished for being what we all desire? It makes no sense."

She swallowed hard, her throat working as her eyes welled up with tears.

Instinct kicked in, and I couldn't help it. I kissed her again, hoping to allay her sadness and fears until David cleared his throat loudly. I lifted my head to glare at him for the interruption.

"We want to hear the rest of the story, remember?" he prompted, one eyebrow cocked at me.

I chuckled and settled back into the couch. "Yeah, yeah, okay." He was right, but now I was hard as a damn rock and couldn't think about anything much other than getting her back into bed as soon as possible.

She smiled, seeming a little happier as her cheeks flushed a cheery pink. "So... anyway," she said, continuing her story. "On my eighteenth birthday, she woke me up in the middle of the night and told me to run. She didn't want my fathers to sell me off to some pack in town that I wasn't a true scent match for."

Anger and relief swirled in my gut in equal measure. Her fathers wanted to sell her off! And then the cold reality of that truth burned a hole in my stomach. If it wasn't for her mother's courage, Tilly would have been mated to some pack in her hometown, not us

Fuck! We'd still be single and lost, probably forever. That was too close a call.

I coughed to clear my throat. "So... you, ah... haven't been home since that night?"

She shook her head. "No," she said emphatically. "Mama told me to never come back, and I knew if I returned, my brothers would probably beat me..." She trailed off when she saw my expression.

I couldn't cope with my mounting anger any longer. I was irate on my mate's behalf and wanted nothing more in the moment than to steal her pain away and make love to her until we were both sated and exhausted. I stood up with ease and scooped her up into my arms as I went.

Her arms slid around my neck, and I groaned as her scent washed over me. She was *so* delicious, I just wanted to bury my nose in her skin and lick her from head to toe.

In fact, I just might do that.

"Where are we going?" Tilly squealed as we made our way toward her nest once more.

I stopped at the base of the stairs, unable to carry her up the ladder-type arrangement we'd had going on for so long as the only access to the loft, which meant we were going to need to install an elevator or remodel to fit proper stairs. When I glanced down at her, her bright blue eyes were lit up with happiness, and my soul sang. I wanted to kiss her until she didn't remember her own name, let alone her horrible past, but I needed to say one thing before I did.

"You know you never have to worry about them again, don't you, beautiful? Your brothers and fathers, I mean? This *whole* town will go to bat for you now that you're one of us. They'll be standing right behind us and Patrick's shield. They won't control you or hurt you ever again."

Real tears shimmered in her eyes this time, and she nodded slowly, wanting to believe it. "Thank you," she whispered.

David had caught up to us now and pressed his lips to the top of Tilly's head with a broad smile on his face. "Are we heading back to her nest?" he asked, unable or not wanting to hide the hope and excitement in his voice.

"Abso-fucking-lutely!" I grinned at him before setting Tilly on her feet and patting her bum until she bolted up the steps with a gleeful squeal. I let David go up to the loft first, so that I had a moment to catch my breath. Not because I was unfit, but because I was still too angry to focus right.

Her brothers and fathers had better not try to claim ownership over her again, because they'd have to get through me first, and I didn't care how many of them there were. She was my mate—*our* mate—and that meant something to us. In fact, it meant everything to us. It meant we'd die—quite literally—for Tilly. And we'd feel the same way until we'd drawn our last breaths. It was a type of loyalty I was certain her fathers had never felt, let alone demonstrated, a day in their lives.

With one last shake of my head clearing my thoughts, I headed up the ladder and into the cozy corner of heaven our mate had created for us with nothing but her love and presence.

CHAPTER FOURTEEN
PATRICK

When Friday morning rolled around, I had the sudden urge to get away and escape the boundaries of our sweet, small town and get a little more wild and remote. We were already awake and organizing breakfast in the kitchen. David was cooking and Michael had our mate pinned to the dining table and was peppering her face with kisses while we waited for crepes again. Matilda loved them, so we weren't going back to our usual bacon and eggs anytime soon.

"Hey, are you guys working this weekend?" I asked, unable to contain the thought any longer.

"Why?" David asked, glancing up from the frying pan.

I shrugged. "I have tomorrow off and most of Sunday too, so I thought maybe we could go away for a few nights. We could stay at the cabin or something?"

Michael pulled himself up so he could join the conversation too. "I could get Bonnie to cover my Sunday shift, and I've got tomorrow off too."

David's eyebrows flicked up then he shrugged. "I never work weekends, you know that, but it's up to Tilly. What do you think, beautiful? Do you want to head to a cozy cabin in the woods for a few days? Or we could fly to Vegas or something more sophisticated if you like? I don't care, as long as we're together."

Michael grinned as he pulled Tilly up into his arms and spoke to her directly. "But you *have* to know… I don't think Patrick has taken a weekend off in twenty years, so this is pretty special."

I rolled my eyes and grabbed a bunch of utensils to set the table. "I take vacations," I remarked under my breath.

"Yeah, when?" Michael demanded to know with a smirk on his face.

I didn't answer. Instead, I finished setting the table and snagged Matilda from Michael's arms. "Come on, baby girl, you need to eat," I said, pulling her seat out for her. She'd put a little weight on this week. I could see it already in her cheeks and her breasts had swelled a little, but she still needed to keep her calories up for her health and strength.

"Oh, yum," she murmured, sitting down and picking up her fork as David simultaneously slid a huge pile of crepes in front of her. "You guys are trying to fatten me up, aren't you?" She laughed.

None of us responded, because it was partly true, but also because there was no safe way of telling a woman she was too thin. In general, it was a dangerous practice to be making commentary on women's bodies, if you knew what was good for you.

She continued once her laughter subsided. "To be honest, it's a bit of a relief. The last pack I dated made me lose fifteen pounds."

David's hiss of anger whistled through the room. "What do you mean, '*made*' you? Why?"

"Is that why you're so thin?" I demanded, sitting down next to her and pouring more sugary syrup over her breakfast. A second later, I regretted letting the words slip from my lips.

She frowned. "I'm not too thin…" she mumbled half-heartedly.

I didn't say anything, instead pressing my lips together so hard, I was fairly sure my nostrils flared in response.

She sighed and put down her fork.

Damn it.

"Okay, I know I'm too thin," she conceded as her shoulders

slumped. "I didn't want to lose that weight, but they wouldn't stop harassing me about losing a size or two, and in the end, it just kind of fell off."

I picked up her fork and handed it to her, hoping my soft smile and raised brows would encourage her. "Stress does that to you, sweetheart. You're still perfect. We just want you to be healthy, happy, and strong. So, please eat. We'd never tell you to lose weight."

"Never," Michael growled in agreement while making himself a plate and sitting down opposite her. His eyebrows were drawn down and together, but he didn't say anything more after that, he just began eating.

Matilda watched him for a time, her lips pursed too, then started eating again, carefully cutting up the crepes, before forking them into her mouth. "So..." she said, clearing her throat once she'd finished her mouthful. "What were you guys talking about? A weekend vacation?"

I shook myself and returned to the original topic of conversation. "Yes. I thought you might want to get away. My treat, of course. I've got the money put aside, and I thought we could all do with some time out. Anywhere you like."

She grinned at me, a sparkle in her eyes. "I've always wanted to see Australia!"

My heart leapt at hearing her making *future* plans with us in mind. "Well, we'd love to take you, but we might need to plan that a little further in advance. We'd have to organize to take a whole month off maybe."

She chewed her bite of food, then swallowed, a more serious expression on her face. "You're... serious?" she asked, a hint of hope at the edge of her tone.

"Of course," I said. "Hell... we can do anything this weekend. I could call the office and see if my deputy can cover next week. Maybe we could do Canada for a bit, or a cruise..."

Did she have a passport? I hadn't thought to ask. But I'd take her anywhere she wanted to go, just as long as we got to love on her all day every day.

She stopped my rambling with the hand she slid over my thigh. "Thank you," she said.

I nodded at her, taking the hint, and waited for her to continue. I'd never taken a girlfriend away for an extended vacation. A dirty weekend maybe, but nowhere meaningful. And now that I had my—our—mate, the options seemed endless. We could do anything. Go anywhere!

Matilda smiled almost apologetically. "But I kind of want to stay home this weekend, if that's okay?"

I frowned at her, taken aback. "Really? The cabin is pretty rustic but modern enough. It has heating and a wood fire and..."

Maybe she thinks I'm trying to take her to some shack with no plumbing?

"Oh, it's not anything like that," she said, accepting the hot chocolate David made for her. "I'm sure it's lovely. I just don't want to be too far from my nest right now. I'm not sure why, but I don't even really want to go out to the diner for that interview yet... which is *weird* for me. I thought I'd be going stir crazy not working by now, but I'm so happy here. Just eating and sleeping and..." She teased her bottom lip between her teeth, then smiled, her cheeks turning a delightful shade of pink.

Fucking?

"Well, if that's what you want," I said, the corners of my lips quirking with the hint of a smile. Our girl was full of surprises.

She nodded emphatically. "Oh, yes, please! We could get takeout and maybe go for picnic or something, but I don't want to go far from home."

Home.

I liked how she said it like that. The way it came to her so naturally, without hesitation or question. I glanced over at the guys. Both were nodding almost as emphatically as Matilda. It seemed they were all down for a weekend at home.

"Well, if that's what you want, baby girl, that's what we'll do."

She grinned and leaned over to kiss me excitedly on the cheek. "It is. Thank you so much for offering though. No one's ever wanted to take me away or spoil me before."

I leaned over and kissed her lips in return because I couldn't cope with thinking about all the assholes she'd trusted before. "You deserve the world," I whispered against her lips before nudging her with my shoulder and returning to my breakfast.

David sat down with his own pile of crepes beside Michael, then cleared his throat. "I was wanting to ask you about your heat suppressors. You picked some up last Saturday, but I wasn't sure if you'd taken them, or if we needed to swap over to another brand or..."

I turned to stare at Matilda, my widened gaze no doubt belying my surprise.

Heat suppressors? Since when?

"Oh..." She started, tripping over her own tongue.

David jumped in to fill the void when he realized his mistake. "I'm sorry, Tilly," he apologized. "I should have asked you privately. That was wrong."

She reached over the table and grabbed his hand to allay his concern. "No. It's okay, I get that you don't want secrets between us. I did take a couple after picking them up last week, because I was fighting my desire after meeting you all. But then Patrick rescued me, and my heat kicked in *so* hard, I thought they weren't working anymore. So, I haven't taken any since. Is that okay?"

"Of course," David said, sounding more professional than warm. "Though you may feel a bit out of sorts this week, and your heat may actually get stronger once the suppressors are completely out of your system."

I practically choked on my coffee. She was going to get *more* aroused and in heat than she was already? I picked up a napkin and dabbed my mouth. "Sorry... you're saying that she could change?" That she was on suppressors when she mounted me in the cab of my truck.

Fucking hell, this is incredible.

We'd already been having sex with her every day, often multiple times. Would she want us even more during her next heat cycle?

David tried not to smile, but I could see the sides of his mouth kicking up. He knew what I was thinking. "Well, not change exactly, but she could certainly feel more passionate going forward, yes."

Michael's laugh bordered on a cackle. "What's wrong, old man? Can't keep up?" he teased, shoving another forkful of crepe into his mouth.

If I wasn't so relieved and happy to know that our mate's need for us wouldn't diminish, I would have clipped the fucker over the back of the head. "Hardly," I managed to say, turning to our mate and kissing her lips. "I've got to get to work, but let's book in some time this weekend to show you off to the world, yeah?"

She nodded, her big eyes growing even larger at the thought of being out in public together officially. "Definitely," she said.

I stood up and just because the desire was still there, I clipped Michael over the back of his head with a grin.

"Hey!" he complained. "What was that for?"

I walked over to the counter and gathered up my sheriff belt, clipping the heavy thing around my waist. "For calling me old," I quipped. "I can still run rings around you, *whipper snapper*." Sure, my hair was graying, and I wasn't as cut as I'd been twenty years ago, but meeting Matilda had me feeling younger and stronger than I had in years.

"Bye, Daddy," she whispered with a little waggling wave as she stared at me with the kind of longing that had me turning hard in one second flat.

I groaned and cussed. "Fuck work."

She giggled but didn't move to jump into my arms or run upstairs.

That gave me a minute to calm myself, take a breath, and drag my arousal down a notch. "God… okay. One more day. See you all tonight."

My pack waved me away, and my mate blew me a kiss.

I headed out into the snow, pulling my hat low. The cold would douse my hard-on for now, but when I got home tonight, I was going to make love to my girl in a way she'd likely never experienced before —slowly and thoroughly—and I'd keep going until she begged me to stop making her come.

Yes. That's the plan.

CHAPTER FIFTEEN
TILLY

A picnic in winter probably wasn't the best idea, but my guys came through, just as I imagined they would. They drove us to a huge park, which featured a large, enclosed rotunda with glass doors and shut us safely away inside, protected from the elements.

To make it comfortable for me, they'd laid down two large picnic rugs on top of the concrete, piled up plush pillows for extra softness, then spread out a delicious buffet lunch, packed in the diner's takeout containers.

"Wow," I whispered as I lounged against Patrick's warm body. With a squishy pillow under my butt, the heavenly aromas of our warm meal and the snow falling outside like a scattered blanket of white, I felt incredibly cherished. "This is amazing, guys."

"Are you sure you don't want to head to Vegas for a late dinner?" Patrick whispered, his breath hot against my ear. "We can make it happen."

I laughed as David picked up one of my feet and moved it to his lap so he could massage it.

God, I'm being spoiled!

"No, this is perfect," I answered. "It's like a dream. In fact, are you sure I didn't die in that snowstorm? Maybe this is Heaven?"

Patrick answered by sliding his hand under my oversized hoodie and cupping my breast. "Does this answer your question?"

I gasped at the unexpected intimacy, then giggled again. "Yeah, I guess that wouldn't be allowed in Heaven, would it?"

Michael, who was lounging nearby, snorted aloud. "Of course it would!" he argued. "What sort of Heaven would it be if you couldn't have sex with your mate?"

"Good point," I said.

Michael sat up and started opening boxes, and the scrumptious aromas filling the rotunda grew even more potent. "Do you want to start with dessert, sweetheart?" he asked as he offered me the ice cream topped cherry pie.

I couldn't help laughing again. "Oh, yes, please."

How does he know me so well already?

My chest and belly hurt because of how much I was laughing these days. I couldn't remember a time when my face would ache from smiling so much. And yet, since meeting my Alpha scent matches, I barely had a moment to feel sad or anything else but blissfully happy and ecstatic.

Honestly, how did I get this lucky?

I took the fork I was offered and ate some of the pie before doing something silly like bursting into tears. I was far too elated to cry, and yet, I wanted to just cry and sob until I passed out. I felt so full of emotions, it was overwhelming. And it was more than a little bit strange not being in fight or flight or survival mode.

I'd done nothing but sleep and fuck and eat all week. It was the closest thing I'd ever known to luxury. But we couldn't continue like this, surely? Perhaps this was like a honeymoon period. Which begged the question, what would normal life look like for us in future? I had no freaking idea. Regardless, it didn't serve anyone to dwell on what might happen. We were here together, and so that's what I decided to focus on.

"This is so decadent," I murmured, gazing over the delicious spread the guys had bought just for me.

David reached out and stroked my hair for a moment without

saying a word, which he did a lot. It seemed like it was a part of his love language. Subtle touches, quiet devotion, cooking our meals... David was so wholesome and gentle it made my heart tangibly ache. As a result, I made sure to brush out my hair every day, just so David could run his hands through it anytime he wanted to.

"It is, isn't it?" Patrick agreed, running his hands over my arms now. "I thought it would be too simple, but it's perfect."

Silence descended again, and I leaned back against his chest once more, loving the heat radiating from their bodies around me. And for the first time in a week my heat felt sated, quiet... happy. So, we ate and chatted about the food, a super contented vibe pulsing among us all.

Is this what it feels like to be part of a real family? To be wanted and loved?

My men wanted me, that much was obvious. And I wanted them, yet I couldn't seem to dredge up the same desire to work or even leave the house. The truth was, I would have still been snuggled up in my nest back home if they hadn't physically carried me to the truck and driven me down here. Did they know how different this all was for me? "You know, I'm not usually this much of a sloth," I said, feebly trying to justify my laziness. "I'm sorry I haven't done anything this week with the house or the cooking or..."

Shit, I've done nothing. Absolutely nothing.

My fathers would have beaten my mother for such a behavior, not that she would have ever risked taking a week off from looking after them.

Patrick's arms wrapped around me, and he pressed his lips to my ear. "What are you talking about?"

David frowned at me. "Yeah, what are you talking about?"

"I've done nothing but sleep *all* week," I said, putting down my empty plate only to fill it with a burger. The guys were right about one thing, at least. I needed to put the weight back on that I'd lost. I had no particular preset ideals about what sexy or attractive looked like, but I wanted to feel healthy and strong again. I was tired of just surviving. I'd done it for years and it was finally my time to thrive.

"Well, that's not true," Patrick said, sliding his hand up to cup my breast again, then growling under his breath.

I smiled, knowing exactly what he meant. "Yeah, but—"

"But nothing," Patrick cut me off, sounding even more daddy Dom than usual. "We don't want a housekeeper, baby girl. We keep telling you that. Just keep resting and taking us to your bed. It's all we want—that and your happiness, of course."

I glanced at the other two men, who nodded and smiled in agreement. I frowned. "So, you don't want me to prepare meals?" I asked.

"To be honest? Not really," David admitted. "I'm already the self-appointed cook of the house. Besides, I like feeding you. I love discovering what you enjoy, and being able to make those things for you makes me happy in turn."

"How about washing your clothes?" I countered, even though David's sentiment and earnest words made my heart melt.

Michael snorted. "Do you want to put poor Nancy out of a job?"

They have a laundry lady? Since when? Damn... I really did sleep too much this week.

"Then what else can I do for you all?" I asked, flummoxed. My mother had been my fathers' slave. She was constantly on edge, always toiling and serving at their leisure.

When Michael's face lit up, I rolled my eyes. "Come on, guys... not just sex." And it wasn't like I was any good at that. At least, I didn't think so, although my men certainly hadn't complained yet. They were insatiable, and every group encounter was a hot, sweaty, and enormously sexy marathon. It was something I hadn't quite processed yet. Why would they want me so much more than anyone else they'd met? I was just me, and aside from the strength I'd taken from my mother's courage to get me out, I'd never thought of myself as anything special. It could only mean one thing. One irrefutable truth, no matter how much I questioned it or didn't understand it.

We really are each other's true scent match.

I just had to trust it and not overthink it. Everything we'd shared together so far had felt right, and they treated me like a modern queen.

Michael swung his huge legs around and sat closer. "Look, beautiful. We just want *you*. You're our someone to love and sleep wrapped around. We've waited years... well, some of us have waited decades, but we won't talk about how old the sheriff is," he teased as he winked at me.

I felt a rumble of vibrations ripple against my back as Patrick growled behind me in response. I grinned and lifted my chin so that I could kiss Daddy.

He kissed me hard, possessively.

They wanted me... my love. I was still struggling with the idea that they desired me at all, let alone the fact they didn't want me to be a slave to them like my mother had been. This was an entirely new story unfolding—one I'd never read before—just for me. I wasn't damned to endure my mother's fate, I was being given a second chance at a real life, one absent of violence and callousness.

When I'd caught my breath, I looked over at Michael. "Okay, but I don't know how to do this. You know that, right? My parents' marriage was very different, and I've never seen a relationship that's very healthy. Not between an omega and a pack of Alphas, anyway." In fact, a pack of three Alphas was almost unheard of.

It happens, but it's rare.

David bent his head and kissed the backs of my knuckles. "Well, let's be the first, then."

My heart exploded in my chest. It was happening. It was real, and I could scarcely believe it. "That sounds really good to me," I answered, unable to hide the emotion in my voice. Wiping away a single tear, I smiled at him and reached for my food. The way they were all loving on me only meant one thing would happen when we got home... and I needed my strength back for another long session of heat-fueled sex. "Aren't you all going to eat?" I prompted, picking up my burger.

Michael grinned, a sexy glint in his mischievous gaze. "Probably should, since we're taking you home to fuck you senseless soon, aren't we?"

I covered my mouth with my hand to suppress the volume of my squeal. "Um, yes, please?"

He grinned and grabbed a strawberry, holding it out for me to bite.

My belly flipped under his gaze and the sensuality that his move suggested. I leaned forward and bit into the plump, crimson strawberry, juice running down my chin as flavor exploded across my tongue.

Michael groaned as though I'd bitten him and not the strawberry.

"Damn, I wish we could just fuck you right here, right now," Patrick growled into my ear.

I giggled and wiped my chin with my hand as I chewed. So did I, in truth. But even as the snow fell steadily, there were still people out walking, and the entire rotunda was made of glass. "Home time?" I asked.

Within moments, the guys were packing up the leftover food, collecting pillows, and folding the blankets.

"Let's go, beautiful," Michael said, grabbing me and swinging me up into his arms before Patrick could reach me first.

"You know I can walk, right?" I asked my big, strong man as he held me close, carrying me into the cold and heading quickly toward the car. We'd brought David's Lexus, his luxury car that had seat warmers and a leather interior. It was *so* nice. I wasn't generally someone who usually gushed over anything so materialistic, but secretly, I loved it.

Michael folded his tall body into the back with me, cradling me practically in his lap, while Patrick and David jumped in the front.

"Home?" David asked, his voice a little deeper and gravelly, the way it went when he wanted to go to bed with me.

I nodded, my heart already racing. "Yes, please." As we sped off, I inhaled their scents around me. In such a confined space with the heater cranked up, my men smelled panty-meltingly amazing. I swallowed the groan that rose as my heat surged within me. My mouth went dry, and my hands felt itchy to the touch. I reached for Michael's arms, gripping his muscles tightly, like they could be my anchors in the maelstrom inside me.

Fuck... I'm wet already.

I clenched my thighs together as they trembled in anticipation of what was to come.

"Oh, sweet Lord," Michael groaned, burying his nose in my neck. "Drive faster, David."

"Do it," Patrick commanded, surprising the hell out of me. "I'll say it's a work emergency if you get a ticket."

David planted his foot, and we sped for home. I would have laughed in exhilaration if Michael hadn't started to kiss and bite my neck. Instead, I arched my back and moved as close to him as I could. Having the local sheriff in the car certainly had its advantages, that was for sure!

CHAPTER SIXTEEN
MICHAEL

*I*f I wasn't so tall, and the car wasn't so fucking small, I would have pulled our mate onto my lap and had her riding my cock all the way home. But until then…

"Oh, God, that feels nice," Tilly murmured.

I ran my tongue around the whorl of her ear and cupped her breast beneath her sweater. Her nipple had pebbled in my palm, and her natural perfume filled the car's cabin. A growl slipped from my throat.

She smells like heaven.

"We're here, hold on!" David called out moments before he swung his car into our driveway.

I braced my arm against the roof and held our mate tight against me. She didn't even seem to notice the abrupt turn, instead she simply melted further into my embrace.

"Let's go," Patrick grunted out, obviously also struggling with the scent of our mate's desire in the car.

I didn't blame him, but God, now that we'd stopped, maybe I could take my cock out of my jeans, and she could just jump on?

Get the party started early…

Both back doors on the car were wrenched open at the same time and clean, fresh air washed through the car. "Out." Patrick demanded, reaching his hand in to escort Tilly from the backseat.

She looked up at me, smiled, then turned to slide out of the car on Patrick's side. "Thank you," she said, her voice sounding husky.

David was at my side, a twinkle of amusement in his gaze. "You didn't think we were going to leave you guys in there to play on your own, did you?"

I pulled myself out the door, unfolding and filling my lungs with invigoratingly frosty air. "No," I conceded ruefully. "But I wouldn't have complained if you had."

David chuckled, and we headed for the front door.

Patrick was already there, letting Tilly's feet hit the ground for a single moment while he wrangled with the door, then before we could even get to them, he had shouldered open the door, picked her up, and stormed the castle with our prize.

I would have laughed whole-heartedly if my balls weren't aching *so* damn badly. We'd all had her last night—all three of us—so how could we want her so desperately again not even twenty-four hours later? Were we ever going to be satisfied? I doubted it. When it came to Tilly, it seemed like no amount of time would ever be enough.

Patrick carried her up the stairs, toward the loft entry. Tilly wanted to be in her nest as often as possible since meeting us, and thanks to David, we now had a proper mattress to sleep on at night. He'd ordered a super king-sized mattress a few days ago, and we now had a comfortable place to sleep that supported us all.

Tilly hopped down and bolted up the ladder to the loft.

Patrick turned to us when we approached. "I think we need to buy a couple more mattresses and frames, maybe connect three together and she could decorate them? The bigger the nest, the better, right? I think Matilda would like that."

"Yeah, maybe," I agreed, then gave him a playful shove. "But that's not what I'm worried about *right now*." I teased. "Get going!"

Patrick grunted at me but did as I suggested and climbed up the steps after her.

When I got to the top of the rungs, I stopped and stared. Tilly was on her makeshift nest, spread out, naked on the mattress. "God, you're perfect," I whispered, walking toward the bed, my cock aching to be free all the while.

Soft sunshine filtered in through the windows despite the cold outside, bathing her in a warm light that enhanced her beauty even more. "Then why are you still over there?" she asked from her place by the pillows.

We had the heaters on, so the room was warm, and yet I didn't feel the need to rush now. None of us did.

"What's wrong?" she asked, sitting up when none of us moved.

Patrick stepped up beside me, also still dressed. "Nothing, baby girl. We're just… enjoying looking at you."

"Hmm," she hummed, running her hands up her sides and cupping her breasts—which were getting fuller by the day. "Okay… but I'm not sure I can wait much longer." Her fingers played with her nipples, then one of her hands dipped down between her thighs, making her gasp as her fingers grazed her clit.

Yep. I'm out.

I reached over my head and pulled my sweater from my body. "Okay, beautiful, you win." My cock bounced out against my belly as I pushed my jeans to the floor and kicked my shoes off. With her pretty painted toenails within reach, and the guys taking their sweet time to undress, I seized my chance and grabbed her ankles, dragging her down the mattress toward me. "I'm going to lick you from head to toe, my girl."

She squealed as I pushed open her legs and crawled over her. Her pussy smelled of sweet vanilla, and I couldn't stop myself from dropping down and licking her wet slit.

She cried out and grabbed onto my head. "Fuck," she breathed.

I'd only wanted a taste, but now that her scent was filling my senses, I settled down on my belly, grabbed her ass with my hands, and decided I was going to eat my fill of her. She screamed out to me as I nibbled at her swollen clit, flicking the fleshy bud from side to side like a menace, triggering wave after wave of pleasure to thrum through her. She bucked against my mouth like a cowgirl riding a bronco, and my cock swelled even further.

Damn, she is so hot.

I couldn't wait a moment longer and I certainly didn't want to. Ready to claim what was mine, I climbed up between her thighs, lined up my cock, and thrust into her slick hole hilt-deep in one fluid motion. Tilly convulsed around me, coming so hard, I almost blew my load right there and then. But I fought the urge back down, needing more.

I wrapped her hair around my fist and covered her with my body, holding her tightly as she trembled beneath me. Then she wrapped her legs around me and drew me deeper still. I flexed my hips and fucked her hard, reveling in the way she clung to me as if holding on for dear life. Her hands were everywhere—in my hair, on my back— her nails digging into my ass as I rode her. With each delicious thrust, I rolled my hips so that my cock almost pulled out of her, then I slid into her *so* deep, I could almost feel her heartbeat like it were my own.

Without any warning, Tilly gasped—her eyes wide—and I realized I was beginning to swell. For the first time ever, I felt a knot developing at the base of my cock. It was a surreal feeling and cock-achingly intense.

Oh, shit... this is new.

But our glorious mate didn't pull away. Instead, she lifted her hips higher, sliding over the thickening knot with urgent desire. Pleasure burst along my cock like internal fireworks as I pushed into her as deep as physically possible. A spasm shivered up my spine, roaring through me as my knot grew, binding us together, flesh to flesh.

"Oh, God!" Tilly cried out, throwing her head back as our orgasm hit us as one.

I growled aloud as my seed pumped into her, my sticky stream flowing longer and stronger than ever before. Tilly spasmed around me all the while, wrapping my cock up in her orgasm and squeezing every inch of me as I filled her up like never before. Our shared climax went on and on, until we could wring no further ecstasy from the moment. I finally collapsed on top of her, my breathing heavy as I quickly flipped us over, so I didn't crush her.

Sprawled on top of me, panting hard, Tilly was delightfully disheveled. "That was incredible," she whispered, resting her head on my chest.

Still inside her, my knot remained swollen, and there was no retreating… not yet. I kissed the top of her head and looked up at Patrick and David, who were nearby and partially clothed. "Um…"

Patrick put up a hand to stop me from continuing, understanding my predicament immediately. "Don't mind us, you enjoy," he said with a warm smirk. "I'm going to go grab a quick, cold shower."

David snorted and threw me a wink. "Yeah, me too. See you in a bit." And then they both disappeared downstairs.

Tilly lifted her head to look straight at me. Her eyes were passion-glazed, and her face was flushed with heat. "That was amazing."

I managed to smile, unfathomably intense feelings of pleasure and possessiveness streaking through me like a rainbow piercing the dark. "It was," I agreed.

She dropped her head once more, resting her face on my chest again, and yawned. "Wow," she said. "I didn't realize how tired I was."

I kissed the top of her head and closed my eyes. "Sleep, beautiful," I coaxed. "We have nowhere to be and you're safe. Sweet dreams, baby." Tilly murmured something I didn't quite catch, then promptly fell fast asleep on my chest.

Was this how it felt to be truly mated? Complete. Whole. Perfect.

I had no idea.

Reaching up, I wrapped my arms around her, holding her close. My mind reeled as my heart raced and my cock pulsed. I never wanted to let her go again.

CHAPTER SEVENTEEN
TILLY

The days faded into one another, like a fantasy dream where I wasn't sure whether I was awake or asleep. Between meals, naps, sex, conversation, and even more sex, time seemed to be disappearing like smoke in a magic trick. My life was amazing.

The guys all worked different shifts, but I almost always had company. I wasn't sure if they'd somehow worked out how to coordinate their schedules to avoid leaving me alone, but if they did, I appreciated it immensely. The house was huge, and I still hadn't moved into my separate bedroom. The space that was mine if I wanted it. I loved the loft and my nest too much to bother. And even though I wasn't nesting as hard as I did when I first moved in, I still preferred to be around my nest, which made me feel safe.

I'd cleaned most of the dust out of the loft now, and we'd set up our enormous nest bed under the window. We had two huge mattresses to sprawl out on, and it was *so* comfy and smelled like the guys. With a million pretty pillows and their clothing that I'd stolen and sprawled near where I slept, it felt like heaven.

And it wasn't like I was all cramped up in there. I had enough room for a full lounge suite, dining table, and bed, and there was an adjoining bathroom too. What else could I possibly need?

Nothing at all.

With a smile on my face, I made my way to the bathroom to use the toilet, glancing at my phone to check the time. It was four o'clock in the afternoon, which meant David would be on his way home, and the house was strangely quiet when empty. Finding no soap on the vanity to wash my hands, I opened a drawer to look for more. I found some tampons and pads that David had probably put in there for me. He'd said he'd set the bathroom up properly for me, and he was seriously the best guy ever when it came to thoughtfulness.

Oh, crap.

The realization suddenly hit me smack in the face as I stared at the sanitary products

When was my last period?

I reached for my phone, logged into my period-tracking app and started scrolling. "Shit," I murmured under my breath. I was late. Only by three days, but I was never late. A second later, I sent David a quick text.

Can you bring a pregnancy test home with you please?

I hit Send, knowing that his pharmacy closed at 4pm, and I didn't want him to miss my message and then have to go back to work to get it. Not only that, but I needed to know if I was pregnant, like... *now.* A weird squeal made its way up my throat, and I slammed my hand over my mouth to stop its escape.

I could be pregnant. Pregnant! How... I can't even!

Oh, I knew how. Of course, I knew how babies came to be, but I just hadn't expected it to happen so quickly for some reason.

Wow... a baby. Their baby! But who's baby is it? Will they care? Will they be happy about it? What should I do first? Go to a doctor? Buy a crib? Sanitize the entire house?

"Seriously, stop. You don't even know if you're pregnant, yet!" I hissed at myself. It felt like I was jumping the gun, so to speak, but I couldn't be that late without a good reason, could I?

Maybe it's just a delayed reaction to weening off my heat suppressors?

My cellphone buzzed in my hand, and I squealed aloud this time, running toward my huge nest and jumping onto the mattress on both knees like an over excited little kid.

Of course, gorgeous girl. Be home in twenty, just have to close up.

I threw myself onto my back, relief coursing over me. He was going to get me the test, and then I'd know for sure, one way or the other. I checked the time again.

Do I have time for a shower?

It would pass the agonizing minutes until David got home, and I was pretty sure Daddy was the only one working late tonight. Snickering, I hauled myself up off the bed and headed to the adjoining bathroom. I'd hoped that washing my hair and making myself lovely and fresh for my men would distract my mind, but the thoughts and questions just kept swirling inside my head.

Should I do the test before Patrick comes home if the other two want me to? Will Daddy be upset if he misses such a big milestone for our pack?

My gut told me yes. He'd want to know, especially since he was the first one to knot me.

Does that mean it's likely that he'd be the biological father? And if he is, will David and Michael care?

In the pack in which I was raised, my fathers had all been brothers who strongly resembled one another, so they hadn't cared who the biological father of any of their children was. They were blood-related no matter what. But David, Michael, and Patrick were considerably different in both their physical appearances and their personalities.

Will they want to do a paternity test and know for sure? Will they all demand a child of their own blood? And does that mean I have to have three children? Damn it, we really should have talked about all this before getting so deep into the relationship.

By the time I'd gotten redressed and noted that my breasts were definitely more swollen and tender than they had been just a few days ago, David arrived home from the pharmacy.

"Hey, beautiful!" he shouted from the front door. "Are you upstairs?"

"Yes!" I called back, racing to the top of my ladder entry. "But I'm coming down. I'll meet you there." I didn't wait for him to respond, instead racing down the ladder and setting off running for the staircase.

David was waiting for me on the landing at the top of the stairs with a paper bag in his hand. "Hey, gorgeous," he said.

"Hi!" I threw myself into his arms, perhaps a little too hard, considering where we were standing.

"Whoa," he said, laughing as he wrapped his arms around me. "Are you okay?"

"Yes," I whispered back, enjoying the way my belly warmed and curled with desire simply from being so close to my incredibly intelligent and caring man. "I just missed you, that's all."

Damn, he smells good.

I dropped my head and inhaled deeply, Filling my senses with his personal scent of apples and cinnamon. It was mouthwatering and sweet and just…

Yum.

"I've got to have a quick shower and wash the day away," he said, gently setting me back on my feet. "Do you want to come and talk to me?"

I nodded, and he held my hand as he led me through his bedroom and into his ensuite bathroom. David was definitely the cleanest of all three of the guys. He showered at least twice a day and always smelled like fresh apple and cinnamon oatmeal crumble, straight out of the oven. Sweet, crisp, and deliciously wicked.

I rested my butt against the bathroom sink while I watched him strip out of his business gear and wash the day away. His hands full of soap suds, he scrubbed his gorgeous body and struck up the obvious conversation. "So… you're late?"

I stood straighter, suddenly feeling as though I were talking to a doctor. "Yes, three days," I admitted, chewing on my inner lip.

"And does your body feel any different?"

I wanted to laugh with anxiety, but he was being *so* sweet! "Yes. My boobs are bigger and a little sore."

He nodded, rinsed himself clean, and turned the water off. "Well, I'm glad you got me before I left, because you definitely sound pregnant."

I nodded, gulping at the lump in my throat. "It's why I wanted to check."

David grabbed a towel and wrapped it around his waist before stepping up to me and putting his hands on my waist. "And how are you feeling about the possibility?" His tenderness was my undoing.

I gulped again, a tear slipping down my cheek unbidden. "I don't know," I said. "It's just so soon. I wasn't really expecting it."

He wiped the tear from my cheek and smiled down at me warmly. "It is. But it seems a natural progression, considering we're all truly scent matched," he consoled me.

I nodded again, momentarily lost for words.

David kissed me gently. "Come sit down and tell me what you're thinking." He led me back to the bed he hadn't slept in since the day I moved in and gestured for me to sit while he went to his wardrobe and grabbed a pair of sweats and a T-shirt. Then he sat beside me, the kindest expression on his face I'd ever seen. "Is this something that you would want to reverse if you could? And that's assuming that the test is even positive."

I frowned, not understanding what he was asking. "What do you mean?" I began. "Reverse?"

"I mean, this is *your* body, beautiful. And even though we'd all be a little sad about putting off having a family, we would absolutely respect your decision if you're not ready."

I stared at him a while longer, waiting for his words to sink in. When they did, I gasped, pressing both palms protectively to my flat belly. "Oh, no," I answered without hesitation. "I would *never* want that. I'm happy! I'm just worried about how you'll all feel about it, that's all."

He grinned at me and pulled me closer, bringing me up onto his lap. "You don't need to worry about us, sweetheart."

I searched his gaze with my own, my heart doing little gallops in the silence that followed. "What do you mean?"

"I mean, we want *you* and we want a family, like, *tomorrow*. The Alpha in me would be so proud to know that we've gotten you pregnant so soon. It means you'll never leave us..." He trailed off, and my heart leapt. For the first time, being *stuck* with a pack felt right. "Sorry," he apologized quickly. "I know I shouldn't say that. Baby or not, you'll never be trapped with us."

I leaned forward and kissed his lips. "You don't need to be afraid of me leaving," I soothed. "I know I've been edgy about losing my independence... but I haven't lost anything and I'm not going anywhere. Every single day since meeting you all has been nothing but gains and blessings." I inhaled sharply, then said something I never thought I'd say. "And right now, I just really need to hear how much you want me."

"Feeling a little fragile?" he asked gently.

It took everything in me not to burst into tears. David was the sort of father I wanted for my babies. He was kind and sweet, and oh, so tender whenever the moment required it. While Patrick would be the strict, no-nonsense daddy, and Michael... well, he'd be all sunshine, ball throwing, and football practices.

"Damn," I wiped at the tears on my cheeks. "I didn't want to cry about this." But the future I was seeing for us all now was just too good not to shed a few tears over.

The dream continues...

"Hey, hey, hey. Are you okay? Are these happy tears?"

I nodded, clutching the small brown paper bag he'd given me. "Can we wait until the guys get home before I test?" I asked. "I think we should all be together if..."

David smiled. "Yeah, of course. There's no rush. Everything is on your timeline, angel. Everything."

I snuggled into my man and closed my eyes, a great sigh escaping me. They'd be home soon enough, and then we'd all know the answer to the only question I had bouncing around in my head right now. Was I pregnant... or not?

CHAPTER EIGHTEEN
MICHAEL

When I got the text from Patrick to get my butt home, I hauled ass, quite literally. A part of me hoped that I knew what this was, but I also had to keep a lid on my expectations. We couldn't possibly have found our omega and gotten her pregnant in a mere matter of weeks, could we?

A few weeks ago, I was working as much as I could and ignoring the fact that I hadn't got laid in forever—and didn't want to. Without the mate bond, my life felt emptier by the day. But not anymore, and now that I'd knotted with my beautiful girl—*our* incredible mate—life was looking rosier than a fucking spring day.

As soon as I opened the front door, I practically raced up the stairs to the loft, taking them two at a time. We may as well have had a studio apartment for all the time we spent in the rest of the house. We had a large four-bedroom house, only for our omega to push us all into the loft? It made me laugh just thinking about it.

As soon as I cleared the stairwell, I saw my mate sitting on Patrick's lap, with David beside her. Panting, I swallowed hard to wet my throat, then took a moment to catch my breath. I wasn't unfit by any stretch of the imagination, but I *had* just run from my truck and sprinted up three flights of stairs. Fueled by excitement and anxiety—

with nothing on my mind but our mate—my head was spinning. "So, where's the fire?" I asked, injecting a splash of humor into my voice.

Tilly stood up and held up a small box, her expression soft but serious. "We wanted to wait for you," she said.

"Is that a pregnancy test?" I ventured. It looked like one, but God knew I'd never seen one up close.

She nodded and worried at her lower lip. "Yeah… I'm already late, and I think I might be pregnant. But I wanted to wait for everyone to be together when I found out for sure."

I walked toward my woman, cupped her face, and kissed her lips, showing her my genuine gratitude. Her taste spread over my tongue, and I couldn't wait to taste her everywhere, all at once.

But later… later.

"Thank you for waiting," I said as I gently withdrew. I wouldn't have missed a moment like this for anything. But now that we're all here, hop to!"

"Okay," she answered, a broad but nervous smile on her face.

When she turned toward the bathroom, I took the opportunity presented and gave her ass a cheeky spank.

"Michael!" she squealed as she ran off to the ensuite and shut the door behind her.

We all stood together, awaiting the news that could change our future. The silence stretched and no one spoke a word. The excitement in the room felt electric yet heavy, like the air before a storm.

Or is it fear?

We hadn't really talked about fatherhood, at least not in any detail. We all wanted kids, I knew that much. But how were we going to navigate co-parenting a baby within a pack dynamic? And what would the baby be? An Alpha, beta, or omega? Boy or girl? The possibilities boggled the mind, but no matter what happened when Tilly revealed her news, we'd handle the situation *together*.

After what felt like an hour, the door opened, and our omega came out, her hand wrapped around a stick of plastic. "I haven't looked yet," she admitted. "I'm too scared."

"Scared of what, beautiful?" I asked. "Of having our baby?"

She bit her lip and shook her head. "No, it's nothing like that. I'm just… I'm nervous. I didn't think this could happen so fast. All of this, right from the start, has just been *really* fast. I kind of feel like I've been swept up in a whirlwind."

Patrick moved toward her, his stoic, calm, and authoritative nature grounding our omega. "It's a good sign, sweetheart, trust me. It means we're compatible."

"I know," she whispered. "But how do you all feel about it? If I'm pregnant, I'm going to put on a lot of weight, and we won't be able to have sex as much. Not to mention, my heat will stop."

Patrick reached out and cupped her face, soothing her with his touch. "You'll be as perfect as ever in our eyes. And nothing on this earth, especially the opinions of others, will stop us feeding and loving you and our baby."

Tilly's eyes sparkled with unshed tears. "Is that how you truly think of the baby?" she asked. "As all of yours?"

Patrick glanced at David then over at me. I nodded in solidarity at our unspoken agreement. "Of course, we do," I told her.

"You don't care about…" She gulped, her gorgeous blue eyes tainted with a hint of fear. "Biology?"

I chuckled and followed up with a quick joke. "Well, we'd obviously prefer if the baby is ours, if that's what you mean?"

Our omega face-palmed and sighed before shaking her head at me. "No, I mean, do you care who the baby's biological father is among you?"

Do we? I don't.

I glanced around at my packmates to see how they felt.

Ever comfortable with taking the lead—even when flanked by another two Alphas—Patrick stepped forward to take her spare hand in his. "Sweetheart, we're a family." He lifted her hand and kissed her fingers. "It doesn't matter whose sperm won the race, we're in this together for the marathon that follows. Diapers to college and beyond."

"Totally," I agreed. "And with the three of us, our baby will be showered with more love, attention, and protection than a kid could ever hope for."

David chuckled. "Same goes for me, gorgeous. All I've ever wanted in life was a family and a mate. And to have an omega true scent match? You're already way past fulfilling even my wildest dreams. A baby would be the icing or the cherry on top of a cake we're all lucky to be a part of."

Tilly's tears spilled down her pale cheeks and she nodded, sucking in a deep breath to steady her nerves. "Okay. Let's all look together." She stepped closer to me, holding her hand out so we could all gather around in a circle. Slowly… so painstakingly slowly, she turned her hand over and opened her fingers up like the petals of a flower unfurling for the sun.

There were no pink lines to decipher or anything to make reading the results difficult. There it was, clear as day, spelled out in digital capital letters.

PREGNANT

"I can't believe it," Tilly whispered, her hand shaking.

David took the test from her grip moments before Patrick swept her up into his arms and twirled her around with a cheer.

"Come here, beautiful girl!" I called out, grabbing Tilly up into my arms and exhaling long and hard. All our dreams were coming true, and I felt like I could breathe again. The anxiety and nerves had been for nothing.

We can do this.

David was next, taking our girl in his arms and holding her tight, he kissed her hair and whispered sweet nothings into her ear.

Patrick caught my eye, and I grinned at him. His face lit up with the biggest smile I'd ever seen on him. Not that it was a cheshire grin by any stretch, but I'd never seen Patrick look so happy. "Does that mean we're moving downstairs and setting up a nursery?" I asked, crossing my arms over my chest. "Or are we selling the house to build the biggest open plan studio apartment ever?"

Tilly stared at me, then clapped her hands excitedly, her eyes as bright as the moon. "A nursery! Do I get to design a nursery?" She almost bounced out of her own skin.

"Of course," Patrick said. "We'll set up a bank account, and we'll all put money in for the baby. You can buy whatever you want or need."

Tilly's face dropped. "Oh, I don't—"

"Stop, baby girl," Patrick said, shushing her as he wrapped his arms around her. "You're carrying our baby, and you're a part of this family now, aren't you?"

She nodded slowly. "Yes."

"Then you're doing the only job you need to do for the time being. You need to rest, eat, grow our baby, and just enjoy this special time. Hopefully, this is just the first of many."

She stared around at us, tears filling her eyes anew, only to slip down her cheeks unheeded. "You're all really happy about this? Seriously? You're not just saying it…"

"Hell, no!" I declared. "This is literally the best news we've ever heard. Like David said, you're our everything, sweetheart, and a baby is the cherry on top."

Tilly began to giggle and then laugh and then the waterworks were set free, and she cried tears of happiness without shame or fear.

David took out his phone. "Speaking of food… I'm going to order some take-out from the diner and go pick it up. We need a celebration dinner where no one cooks or cleans. What do you think, beautiful?"

Tilly nodded. "Oh, yes please. I just want to climb into my nest with all three of you and never leave." And she meant it. "But…" She stared at David, her lips turning down briefly. "We haven't knotted yet. Does that mean anything?"

David shook his head, a broad grin on his face. "Nothing at all, baby. Well, if anything, it just means it's my turn next!"

She laughed and ran at him, wrapping her arms around our smart friend. David returned the hug, closing his eyes in what looked like sweet relief.

I grinned myself, the joy contagious. "All right, well, I'll go make us some drinks. David, Patrick, beer? Beautiful, peppermint tea?"

Everyone nodded and offered their thanks, so I headed to the kitchen while David called the diner, and Patrick settled our mate back into her pile of pillows and pretty blankets. Nothing had felt this good, *ever*. We were on the right path now, and I never wanted to leave it. My thoughts whirred and my heart sang, but one truth stood out against all others and rose to the forefront of my mind.

I'm going to be a father!

I could barely believe it.

CHAPTER NINETEEN
TILLY

My stomach lurched with the familiar feeling of morning sickness. It'd hit me hard a week after first discovering I was pregnant, and the only things that seemed to help were ginger biscuits and peppermint tea. I reached for the mug of peppermint tea Michael had made for me earlier and took a few calming sips.

Ugh, this sucks.

Patrick bent his head down to kiss me on his way to work, then turned around in his tracks. "Hey, beautiful. Can I ask you something?"

"Of course," I answered, loving the way that my Daddy mate spoke to me.

He tilted his head a little, his lips pursed as though he were deep in thought.

"Whatever it is, it looks serious," I said, shifting on the cushion I'd propped myself up on in order to get more comfortable.

He stepped back toward me. "I was just thinking… now that you're pregnant, I'd like to register our relationship with the Omega Registration Board. What do you think?"

I stiffened.

Crap. He wants to own me. They all do.

I should have known this was coming, but I'd been ignoring the fact that my new pack would want to do this. I was surprised and couldn't help but feel annoyed. "Why?" I asked Patrick as he pulled on his jacket to head out the door. "Do you need the money that badly?"

I knew they'd doubled the omega payment to packs last year, and it was up to over twenty thousand dollars now. And I was quite sure sheriffs didn't get paid all that much.

He can't want to own me so badly that he'd put a price on me like that, can he?

Patrick froze just as he slid his cell phone into his pocket, then he turned on his heel to growl at me. "What did you just say?"

I swallowed in the face of aggression. I hadn't meant to say it quite so harshly. Maybe I wasn't over my past traumas as much as I thought. And maybe my hormones were running amuck, but this whole happy family thing was still *very* new to me. "Um..." I couldn't find the words.

Patrick walked over to the combined mattresses that we slept on, sat down, then patted his lap. "Come here, baby girl."

I reacted on instinct, no thought involved. There was nothing but an all-consuming desire to obey, and a raw need for comfort and physical affection. I scrambled to get to him, practically curling up in his lap like a content house cat, but inside, my stomach roiled.

Oh my God. He's upset with me.

I didn't think that I could deal with an argument or admonishment in my current state. My stomach twisted and it felt worse than any morning sickness I'd experienced so far.

When he set his arms gently but possessively around me, I clung to him like a limpet to a rock, burying my nose into his neck so that I could inhale his scent. My hammering heart began to slow, but my lungs burned. I couldn't breathe whenever Patrick was upset with me. I craved his special brand of seductive authority and affection. Being without it was like being denied the sun's light.

"You know that I love you, right?" Patrick said.

I nodded, sliding my arms around his neck. I did know that he loved me and that he wanted what was best for us. But that didn't mean that I wanted to totally give up all control entirely, and I certainly wasn't going to stop asking questions. My mother didn't raise a doormat. She set me free from the bonds of the past. It would be a sickening betrayal of her memory if I gave myself up to live life as nothing more than a domestic slave.

"Then you need to know that I'd never take money that was rightfully yours," he continued.

"Mine?" I repeated, lifting my head so I could look at him. "My dads always said that money was meant to go to the pack. To the men who had to put up with the burden of having an omega." The anger and hatred I felt in that moment shocked me and I had to look away from Patrick's handsome face to cough and clear my throat. Those bastards had made me feel worthless my whole life. Worse than worthless.

And yet they relied on my mother for all the housekeeping, shopping, and cooking. Not to mention the exhaustive labors of child rearing and keeping three men sexually satisfied. But she was worthless?

Anger rose at the hypocrisy of it all. They were all liars… liars!

They can all get fucked. Seriously.

Patrick sighed and ran a hand through my hair. "Baby girl, that money is for you, if you want it. Or you can put it into the account we created for the baby. It's not mine or David's or Michael's. As the name implies, the omega payment is for the benefit of the omega. It's for whatever you need to settle into a committed relationship within a pack."

"Oh." A fleeting blush of shame flooded my cheeks. I'd thought he was angry. That they all just wanted to make things official for money —like my old packs would have—but all he wanted to do was help me get what I was entitled to. My mind boggled. I'd never even wondered what I'd do with that amount of cash. It was *so* much money, especially when I'd never had more than a meager figure in savings to rely on.

Patrick cleared his throat. "And I shouldn't have to say it, but I will. Your fathers were wrong."

Sucking in my lower lip, I fought back a hiccup as my breathing became momentarily erratic. I was starting to agree with him. As I was growing up, I'd genuinely thought omegas were trash. That any of us were lucky to not be out on our asses. But once I was out on my own, I'd learned a *different* truth. A pack needed an omega as much as we needed them. Our societal structure followed our natural instincts, cycles, and desires. But somewhere along the way, everything had become twisted and warped by the heavy hand of old-fashioned Alphas.

Why did I keep sinking back into that old way of thinking?

"Very wrong," Patrick reiterated, breaking into my thoughts. "You, my baby girl, are a blessing to me and our family. You make us a family, Matilda. You turn this house into a home. Promise me that you'll never forget, okay?"

I nodded but said nothing, still lost in a storm of emotion and increasingly frustrating need. Sitting on Patrick's lap always did this to me. Aching for him even as he was concentrating on nothing more than this deep conversation, it was almost funny.

He raised an eyebrow at me, and I giggled. "Yes, Daddy," I whispered. It felt so naughty to call him that, but also incredibly hot. His scent, combined with the chaos of my hormones, made me wickedly horny.

And speaking of horny...

I wriggled in his lap and smiled from under my lashes.

Patrick groaned. "Please don't tempt me. My shift already started five minutes ago."

"Aw!" I laughed as I hopped off his lap, feeling light and happy, as if my mood were a puppet that could be made to dance and jump from stress to levity.

He got to his feet and adjusted his pants. "Damn. You get me harder than steel in seconds, you know that?"

I pouted and groaned. "Don't tell me that," I sulked, feeding the urges growing inside me again. I was unbelievably tempted to just go down on my knees and take his cock out to suck. He had an amazing cock. The length, thickness, and overall attractiveness was undeniable. I didn't like to pick favorites, but Daddy's was seriously fucking delicious.

I must have sighed in need or stared too long at the object of my desire, because Patrick started unzipping his pants before I could even utter a word. I went down on my knees and immediately joined him in pulling open his trousers. His cock bounced out, girthy and long. The head was so exquisitely shaped. It reminded me of an arrowhead.

I wrapped my hand around his stiffening shaft, loving the way the soft pink was darkening to a blush red. I hummed aloud as I wrapped my lips around him and trailed my tongue along the underside of the head.

"Damn, baby girl. You are too hot," he growled, watching me with sinfully delicious intensity.

I wanted to be. For him, I wanted to be everything he'd ever wanted. Pleasing him was an addiction, and his praise was the salve for all my wounds. I pumped my hand up and down the shaft until I felt a sweet sting dance across my scalp for the briefest of moments. I paused and looked up, my entire focus on him.

"Fuck, I need you," he groaned as he tangled his hand in my hair.

Inspired, I deep throated him once more before coming off him with a wet suck and a distinctive *pop*. "Do you?" I asked, my heart in my throat as my pussy began to ache.

He pushed me onto the bed, and I fell back with a laugh. "Flip over. Ass up. Panties off," he commanded.

Luckily for me, I was wearing a long skirt, so I pushed my underwear off, rolled over, got up on my hands and knees, and threw my skirt over my head, presenting boldly for him.

Daddy slid his fingers between my thighs and moaned deep in his throat, finding me already wet and ready for him. "God, you're so hot, baby."

"Please, Daddy," I panted, pushing back against his probing fingers. I was aching terribly, needing him inside me. "Fuck me!"

Without further prompting, Patrick lined up, set the head to my opening, grabbed my hips, and growled again. "With pleasure, sweetheart." Then he plunged deep inside me.

"Oh, God. Yes!" I cried out as I reached for an anchor, fisting the blankets in my attempt to hold on while a storm of ecstasy whipped through both of us. The sex was fast and hot, and he fucked me so hard that I came in mere moments, calling out *"Daddy!"* at the top of my lungs as I climaxed.

"Fuck!" Patrick toppled after me, crying out with his release.

I collapsed onto the bed as he slid out of me, laughing and sobbing with sweet relief.

How is this my life? It's just too good to be true.

"Girl, you'll be the death of me."

I rolled onto my back, slick between my legs and barely able to wipe the smile from my lips. "What a great way to go," I said, stretching luxuriously in my postcoital bliss. Though the idea of losing Patrick made me feel literally sick, so I banished the thought from my mind.

He grinned as he zipped his pants back up and readjusted his shirt. "Happy?" he asked.

"Hmm…" I responded as I reached for a pillow to cuddle at the same time he slipped a blanket over me, making me warm. I was going to pass out again. My pregnant body needed a surprising amount of rest. Already feeling the physical symptoms of fatigue, I closed my eyes.

"So, are you okay for me to call in the omega mating?" Patrick asked.

I nodded with a breathy sigh. This was obviously important to him, so why would I fight it? No harm would come of it, but my curiosity needed sating. "Of course," I said. "But why does it matter to you so much?"

He shrugged nonchalantly. "Well, number one, it'll give you some cash for baby items and a new car. I know you're not thrilled about letting us buy things for you."

I chuckled because he was right about that. I loved that my men wanted to look after me, but I had rejected their efforts to buy me practically anything since we'd met. I didn't want to rely on my pack to survive. That would put me in a situation far too similar to my mother's for me to be comfortable.

"Well… maybe I could put the money into that account you guys want to set up for the baby, like you said before." Having a good chunk of cash in an account, just in my name, sounded like heaven. Or better still, it sounded like the freedom to choose. It was the gift, the *right* and access to choice, and that's all I'd ever wanted.

Patrick groaned as he picked up his cell phone. "Give me two secs, okay? I have to let Toby know I'm late." He tapped a message into his phone, then grabbed his keys.

When he kissed me, the taste of honey was strong.

Hmmm… he truly is divine.

"Was there another reason?" I managed to ask as he walked toward the ladder that led down into the house and out of the loft.

"Hmmm?" he hummed.

"You said number one, but there wasn't a number two." People generally only did that when there was a larger list to talk about.

"Well…" Patrick stopped to put his sheriff's hat on. He seemed to be hesitating and delaying his answer.

Maybe I shouldn't have asked?

I was just so tired. Maybe I'd just close my eyes… and…

"Once we register our mating, we can get married," he said finally, his voice breaking through the first fluttering of sleep's kiss.

My eyes popped open. "We… you…" I trailed off, unable to cobble my thoughts together. Physically shaking slumber's touch off, I sat up, my wonderful bliss forgotten. My heart began to pump loud and hard in my chest.

Did he kind of just…

He held up both hands in a defensive, halting gesture. "This is *not* me proposing," he clarified with a wry smile. "The guys would have my fucking head if I dared to do it without them, but how would you feel about being ours forever, baby girl? Do you want to get married at some stage? Hypothetically speaking?"

I wanted to squeal with excitement and nerves but managed to just smile like a love-struck idiot. It was obvious the guys had been talking about it, and I didn't want to ruin their surprise in any way. Besides, I loved the fact that he respected my desire to question, answered truthfully, and wanted to check with me first before they even officially asked. It showed a level of trust and understanding that my fathers would never have had the decency to show my mother. In fact, I was pretty certain my parents weren't even married. They were just mated—bonded.

Like a servant and master.

I shook my head to clear the ugly thoughts about my mother's relationship with her Alphas and nodded. "I'd be very open to that possibility. I'd never really thought about it much before, given my circumstances. But yes, I think it's a great future idea."

Patrick put his finger to his lips and whispered, "It's our little secret, yeah? I just had to be sure."

"Yes, Daddy." I whispered back and nodded. This time around, I couldn't help but utter an ecstatic little squeal.

Daddy winked at me and tipped his hat, then headed down the ladder to go to his office in town.

Married! Me? I can't believe it.

I collapsed back onto the mattresses and closed my eyes. They wanted to marry me! What we had was so much more than even a true scent match bond. It was a relationship between the four of us that they saw enduring through all the years of their lives. I just… I couldn't believe it!

The next thing I knew, my alarm on my phone went off, and I reached for the obnoxious noise. Silencing it, I checked the time. I'd gotten a couple of hours sleep and felt better for it, but I needed to get up and get ready. It was almost time for the interview my guys had set up for me before we knew I was pregnant. Even if it ended up only being a viable option for a few months, I still wanted to work. I could save some pocket money to treat myself with after the baby was born. And anyway, getting closer to Michael's sister, the future auntie of our child, seemed like a good idea to me.

CHAPTER TWENTY
DAVID

I arrived home and found Michael painting the kitchen. He stood on the ground, wielding a long pole with a roller attachment so he could give the ceiling a fresh coat from the looks of it. "What are you doing?" I asked, sliding my keys onto the hook next to the fridge.

Michael snorted and rolled his eyes. "What does it look like?"

I rolled my eyes right back. "I know you're painting, but why? And has Tilly picked a room for the nursery yet?"

He shook his head and grimaced. "Not yet, which is why I'm doing this. I'm just wasting time, refreshing the place until she does. I'm going insane without her here. I really loved having her around more often." He put his massive roller down and dusted his hands off. He had a splotch of white paint on his shirt, and I wasn't going to tell him. Frustration rolled off him in waves, and I wasn't getting caught in that trap.

"I'll bet you did." I snorted. "Well, do you want to go down to the diner for dinner then?" It was only five o'clock, but I wasn't in the mood to cook, especially if my only company was going to be pissed off the entire time. Plus, we'd get to see our mate, and that'd hopefully remedy Michael's shitty mood.

Michael's eyes widened as he finished dusting off his hands. "Hell, yes. Just give me ten to shower and change." He left the kitchen and ran off up the stairs like a kid who was just promised candy. The chance to see Tilly was clearly inspirational.

I glanced at the mess and the paint my pack brother had left behind and didn't even care that I was caretaking and cleaning up after everyone again. I was far too happy to worry about any of that inconsequential shit. I popped the roller in a bucket of water to soak in the laundry tub and threw everything else in the garage.

Tilly had started working at the diner a few weeks ago, and everyone loved her.

Unfortunately.

She accepted way too many shifts, and we were constantly at home without her now. It had been three weeks since Toby had given her the job, and it sucked. Especially with her finally feeling better after her initial sojourn with morning sickness, I desperately wanted to spend more time with her.

But how do we do that?

We needed to organize a family meeting, that was the only answer. We had to open the lines of communication, compromise, or both. One of us, or all of us, was going to have to drop down to part-time hours, or we'd never see our mate. Michael still wasn't downstairs yet, so I glanced at my phone and messaged Patrick.

What time do you finish? We're going to the diner for dinner.

He responded immediately.

Shift doesn't finish until midnight, but I'll try to pop in for some food around 6pm.

I slid my phone back into my pocket.

Perfect.

Michael was still in the shower, so I went to my room to change shirts while I waited, but when I got there, I realized I didn't want to go and see my gorgeous mate with the smell of the day on me. So, I stripped off and had a quick shower and a shave, then put on a fresh pair of jeans and a casual T-shirt, a rarity for me. Thankfully, by the time I got back to the kitchen, Michael was finally ready too, so we could go.

"I'm driving," I said, grabbing my keys and heading out the front door again.

"No argument here," Michael said and proceeded to vibrate with excitement all the way to the diner.

When we got out of the car, I glanced at him and sighed. I needed to be real. "I think I need to hire another pharmacist or something. I hate never seeing Tilly anymore."

Michael laughed, but his expression was empathetic and understanding. "I'm already doing the same thing. In fact, I'm thinking of getting into property development and handing over more of the motel's responsibilities to Hollie."

I opened the glass door, and we walked into the diner. It was good to know I wasn't alone in how I felt. "Sounds like we've been thinking the same thing."

"Yeah," Michael agreed with a grunt. "Less work and more time for fucking, fun, and family!"

I couldn't help myself. I laughed aloud and shook my head with mirth. "Now that's a family motto we should put above the front door!"

Michael grinned at me. "I reckon."

A moment later, Jessica, one of the waitresses, walked up to greet us. "Hey, guys. Are you here for dinner?"

I nodded. "Yes, please. And I think Patrick's going to pop in too."

She smiled and grabbed the menus. "Come on then. I'll seat you in your mate's section."

Our mate. Damn, that sounds nice. But not quite right either...

"Here you go." Jessica pointed us to a large booth and placed the menus on the table.

I slid onto one of the leather seats while Michael took the other. "Where's Tilly?" I asked.

Jessica grinned. "She's in the kitchen but won't be long."

As if her words had conjured our lovely mate, Tilly came running over to us. Her cheeks were flushed a rosy pink, and she grinned from ear to ear. "Hey, boys," she said, lifting her pen and pointing it toward the pad of paper. "What can I get you?"

"A kiss for starters," I said, reaching out for her and pulling her into the booth with me.

She squealed to get away but kissed me anyway. "I'm working!" she complained, though the smile on her face never wavered.

Michael ordered a burger and pie, and I did the same. "Thanks, beautiful," we both said at the exact same moment.

Tilly giggled and went to walk away but turned back to kiss Michael too before hurrying away to the kitchen once more, her blonde ponytail swinging happily behind her.

"Damn, she's perfect," Michael said as we watched her bustle away.

"I know," I agreed, shaking myself just so I could look away once more. "I'm not sure how we got so lucky but—"

"Don't care," Michael interjected. "She's ours and that's all that matters."

"Sure is." I changed the subject back to the plans Michael mentioned earlier at home, and we talked house prices and renovations before our mate brought our food to the table. "Do you still finish at eight?" I asked, pulling my plate closer and inhaling deeply.

Tilly nodded. "Yep! My feet are absolutely killing me."

"How about a bath when we get home, baby?" Michael offered not entirely innocently.

Our mate grinned at him. "Oh, yes. Definitely," she purred, biting her lower lip.

I couldn't stop the flutter of lust that stirred in my belly at the mere hint of intimacy, nor did I want to. We all *knew* what happened after a bath. Tilly was so stunning when she was naked, especially with the little bit of weight she'd put on recently. Her hips and her lush ass were enough to make me growl with need. "Grrr…" I shook myself and cleared my husky throat. "Bring on home time!"

She laughed then turned toward the sound of the tinkling bell that rang over the diner's front door.

"What's wrong?" Michael asked, turning toward the intrusion too.

Tilly's lovely, once joyful face drained of blood in a single heartbeat. She was white as a sheet and looked like she was on the edge of bursting into tears. And just like that, the perfect life we'd been living shattered like glass at our feet. The past had finally caught up with our mate. "Um…" she breathed, still as a statue. "They're my dads, and…" She gulped as the bell rang again, signaling another round of people had entered the restaurant. "My brothers."

I looked toward the door and saw the men she was staring at with horror. There were eight men in total. Four of them were about our age, and the other four appeared to be in their sixties. They looked disheveled, tough, and more than rough around the edges. They reeked of violence. Tilly made a barely audible whimpering noise, her heart in her throat as she took a cautious step back. "Go to Toby, sweetheart. Now. We've got this."

She met my gaze, her eyes glistening, nodded and turned tail and ran.

Good girl.

I saw two of the younger men step forward as if to chase her, then stop and clench their fists in a rage when she disappeared behind the counter and through the double doors into the kitchen out back.

"I'm calling Patrick," Michael said, his phone already at his ear.

I nodded at him and slid out of the booth to get to my feet. "Do," I agreed. "And tell him to bring *everybody*." We were majorly outnumbered, and my heart pounded with the adrenaline and rage I needed to survive the fight to come. These men had made Tilly's life a living hell until the day she'd turned eighteen and fled. As I stood holding my ground, I lifted my chin in subtle masculine acknowledgment of their presence. One thing was for damn certain—they weren't getting through me. And they weren't touching our fucking mate.

Michael was on the phone talking to Patrick under his breath, but I didn't dare take my eyes off the intruding pack of men. The diner had a back entrance as well as a second floor. But a pregnant omega, especially one that had a scent they were familiar with, would be impossible to hide, so that idea was out the window.

Taking a step forward, I decided I would try to talk to them and see what they wanted. After all, I was a peaceful man at heart. But they didn't look peaceful and they sure as fuck didn't look like they wanted to just talk. I'd always try to reason my way out of an unpleasant situation first, but if the fight was on, we'd do *anything* to protect our mate. And if this was going to get ugly, it was going to get ugly really fast.

I just hope Patrick and the cavalry aren't far.

CHAPTER TWENTY-ONE
TILLY

"Oh, crap. Oh, crap. Oh, crap," I muttered under my breath as I shook like a leaf, huddled up beside the main cook and the owner of the diner, Toby.

"How many of them did you say there were?" he asked, cracking his knuckles.

I bit my lip and squeezed my fingers tighter around my arms to steady myself. "My four brothers and four fathers."

Toby untied his apron and threw it on the counter, full of courage. "I have to get out there," he told me.

"No. Please don't leave me," I whimpered. "David told me to stay with you."

Toby frowned. "I know, but it's two against eight out there, Tilly. I can't leave them. I have to help."

I trembled again, willing myself to be steadfast in the face of the terror of my past colliding with my hopes and dreams for the future. "You're right," I agreed despite my fear. "Go. Please."

Please don't let my mates get hurt.

My brothers were big bastard bullies, and my dads were aging but still mean to the core. This could get bad fast.

"I'm here!" Hollie exclaimed. She rushed over and wrapped her arms protectively around me, holding me close.

Best future sister-in-law ever.

I let my arms drop from where they were wrapped around my torso, then slid them around Hollie. She was my strength now, because in the face of my past, I had nothing. Instead of the loved, independent woman I'd become, I felt like an unwanted little girl again. "I'm so glad you're okay," I said, swallowing hard.

"Who are those guys?" Hollie asked me.

She didn't know and she came to help me anyway...

"My dads and brothers," I whispered.

Hollie pulled back a little, and I looked up to see concern in her face. She didn't know my history, obviously. I hadn't shared that part of my life with her, and it seemed that her brother hadn't filled her in, either.

"Michael never told you anything?" I asked.

Her frown deepened and she shook her head. "Um, no... Why would he?"

I sighed and pulled back as a strange numbness settled over me. "My fathers wanted to sell me off to a pack in my hometown as soon as I turned eighteen, and my brothers always harassed me. It wasn't quite outright abuse, but it was *very* close to it."

Hollie growled low in her throat, took my hand, and dragged me to the swinging door of the kitchen so that we could look through the glass porthole and back out into the diner.

I gasped aloud in panic, quickly plastering my hand over my mouth. Michael and David were facing off against a solid wall of my angry family members.

"We need to get out there," Hollie hissed under her breath. "Those odds are not good."

My phone buzzed in my back pocket, and I grabbed for it. "I hope it's Patrick." It was.

I'm five minutes out.

"Shit. We need to stall them." I grimaced as I showed Hollie the text. "We need a diversion or something!"

She nodded, as brave as her brother. "A diversion, you say? Okay. Let's go see if they want something to eat or drink at our fine establishment while they're here." She picked up her tray, plastered on a grin, and went out through the door like an absolutely bold-as-brass queen.

I watched on with bated breath, biting my lip as she walked up to the group and started trying to talk them into sitting down. "Please be safe," I whispered, bouncing on my toes as my whole body zinged with adrenalin.

One of my dads took a swipe at her. "Stupid bitch," he swore.

But Michael was faster. He grabbed his sister as she stumbled back, catching her before she could fall to the floor.

And just like that, a rage unlike any I'd ever known exploded inside me.

How dare he lay a finger on her!

I pushed through the swinging door and stormed up to the men who were now my enemies. "What the hell do you want?" I demanded, hands clenched into white-knuckled fists at my sides.

Dad Number One blinked at me while some of my brothers actually took a step back. Dad Number Two growled, "We got a letter in the mail from the omega association saying you're getting mated. But that can't be right. You know you were promised to a pack back home. You've got to honor the arrangement."

Fuck. Stupid fucking council. How dare they send my fathers a letter with my current details?

I rolled my eyes and put my hands on my hips in the hope that I'd look stronger than I felt. "It's been five years," I argued back. "Haven't they found another omega by now?"

From the way they looked at each other, I guessed not. Didn't say much for the quality of the pack, did it?

Dad Number Three stepped closer and tried to grab my arm. "Come here," he grumbled.

I evaded him and glared at him with all the courage I had in my heart. "Don't you *dare* grab at me like that ever again. I'm not yours to control. Not anymore." My chest flared with heat as I stood my ground. I was angry, but we were supposed to be creating a diversion to buy us time until Patrick arrived with backup. I had to keep them talking.

Dad Number Two snorted derisively, the sound meant to cut me down like a knife. "Bullshit, girl. You're ours—always have been—and now that we've found you, you're going to mate with whoever-the-fuck we say."

"We don't think so," Michael said, stepping up beside me as David moved to my right. "She's ours."

One of my brothers laughed. "Look at these dickheads," he scoffed. "Who do they think they are?"

"My true scent matches," I said with conviction, lifting my chin. "And I've already agreed to the mating. I can't undo it nor do I want to." Neither of my men were touching me, which felt strange, but they appeared tense and ready to spring into action if necessary.

We just needed a few more minutes.

"Look, there's history here, and emotions are high. Why don't you sit down and have a coffee with us?" David offered. "It's on me. After all, we'll be family soon." As the calming influence of our pack, he was trying to placate them—I could see that—but he didn't realize that my fathers weren't used to or fond of men who had more money than they did. In fact, it was the surest and fastest way to get their tempers flaring to nuclear levels.

Shit!

"I don't fucking think so!" Dad Number Four yelled, charging right at me. He seized me by the arms and hauled me against him. "You're coming home with us. *Now.*"

"No!" I screamed with a mother's wrath as I fought to get out of his grip. I could have told them I was pregnant and hope for the best. For a split second I considered it, but I wasn't certain that it would keep me safe. Instead, it could find me being punished in the worst possible way. My heart physically ached in my chest at the mere thought of it.

I need to keep our baby safe... no matter what it takes.

And just like that, any hope for peaceful negotiations died as a huge brawl broke out around us. Seeing their mate being manhandled in front of their very eyes, David and Michael started swinging at my brothers. While my mates faced off against them, all four of my fathers worked together to carry me toward the front door.

I heard my name hollered and wrenched my neck backward to see. It was Hollie, trying to get through the melee to reach me. Toby had joined the fight too. The three of them were trying to knock my brothers out of the way, but it was already too late, and they were pulled back into the fray. The bell above the front door rang as we burst through, the metallic sound like that of a guillotine to my ears—the sound of the end. "No!" I screamed again, bodily fighting and kicking at my four fathers.

"Shut the fuck up!" Dad Number One yelled at me. "Or I'll shut you up myself." He raised his arm, showing me his clenched fist.

I could handle a punch and had before. At worst, it might knock me unconscious, but would my pregnancy survive a trauma like that? I was only ten weeks along and had no idea how stable it was. My first sonogram was still two weeks away. It was something we had been looking forward to, counting down the days like real first-time parents together. "Okay, okay," I agreed, gulping back the tears and fear that rose as I forced my body to relax and comply with my will. "I'm sorry. I won't fight you."

"Make her walk," Dad Number One said.

A heartbeat later, I was basically dropped to the sidewalk like a discarded rag doll. I tumbled to my hands and knees on purpose, falling as carefully as possible while grappling with the instinct to grab for my stomach to protect my precious baby.

Don't give yourself away. Stay focused.

"Get up!" he barked at me, his voice filled with loathing and barely contained rage. "Walk!"

"Coming!" I answered as pleasantly as I could muster, in automatic survival mode. It frightened me how easily I could slip back into my old skin, into that of a girl with no hope. My heart pounded in my chest like a steam locomotive rattling the tracks. Then the sound of breaking glass reached my ears as someone from inside the diner threw a chair into the window. One of my fathers grabbed my arms and roughly hauled me to my feet.

"Hurry up. Get her in the car." He shoved me toward the old truck, and I stumbled, my feet like lead.

I have to run or fight—now.

If they got me in the truck, I was done for. I'd never see my men again, and our baby… I gulped in the brisk air, and it seared my lungs. I kept my eyes on the ground, readying myself to make a run for it. My odds weren't terrible, but they weren't great by any stretch of the imagination.

Michael and David were still fighting with my brothers inside, and no one had emerged from the diner yet. My dads were cruel and strong, but they were old, and I was fast when I needed to be. Mercifully, I was wearing good sneakers and I knew the parking lot and the surrounding streets like the back of my hands, all advantages over my dads.

"Move it!" Dad pushed me in the back, and I stumbled properly this time, landing on my knees once more.

I have to run. I have to take the chance.

I clenched my hands into fists on the ground and spotted a gap between two of my dads, so I took it. I launched myself to my feet and bolted forward, the fear of recapture spurning me on, and that's when the sirens sounded. Patrick's black truck swung into the parking lot, stopping hard in front of me. With my heart in my throat, I ran straight for him, a choked sob escaping me as tears turned icy on my cheeks.

The sheriff threw the door open and jumped out, wrapping one arm around me as he lifted his gun against my fathers with his other. "Freeze!" he boomed over the sirens as two more sheriff's cars pulled up.

Two deputies got out, long guns aimed over their doors, straight at my fathers. They were not fucking around.

I sobbed as I buried myself into Patrick's shoulder, inhaling his delicious, familiar scent to calm my frantic heart.

"Sorry I was late," he said, gripping me hard. "Are you hurt?"

I shook my head. "No… no…I'm…" I looked back at my tormentors, and my dads all stood stock still.

The glass doors to the diner burst open a moment later, and people poured out. David and Michael came straight toward us, elbowing my fathers out of the way.

Michael reached for me, and I went to him, gasping loudly. "Oh my God. You're hurt!" I lamented, my brows scrunching in empathy and concern. His lip was split, and his right eye was almost swollen shut. But David fared the worst.

My poor men.

"We're fine," Michael said dismissively, gathering me close. "But we better get you to the hospital for a check-up."

"Me?" I scoffed. "You need stitches!" And they did. Their injuries were significant, and the blood wasn't stopping. David's whole left side of his face was red and the skin was broken, but he was standing while my brothers were nowhere to be seen.

"Take our mate to the hospital," Patrick instructed without looking our way. "Make sure our baby is okay, get your face stitched up, and meet us at the station."

"She's pregnant?" Dad Number Two spat. "You little whore!"

The insult fell on deaf ears. The sheriff wouldn't even dignify them with a response. Instead, he just did his job. "You're all under arrest."

David took my hand and led me toward the ambulance that had pulled in behind Patrick's truck. In short order, I was bundled up with a blanket and taken to safety. As I lay down on the gurney with two of my pack by my side, I rested my hands protectively over my soft belly. And for the first time in my life, I *finally* felt like I could breathe.

CHAPTER TWENTY-TWO
PATRICK

After more than four hours grilling the eight gorillas who comprised Matilda's family and charging them with attempted kidnapping and assault, I was still fucking fuming. I didn't even remember the drive home, but once there, I jumped out of the truck, slammed the door, and ran up the steps into the house. I'd never been so grateful to be part of a pack in my life. Knowing my mate was safe with the two men I trusted most in the world, well… it made it okay for me to be the angry one, because she was safe.

Michael came around the corner to greet me at the front door as I shook the rain off my coat. "Shhh… she's sleeping," he warned me.

I nodded but didn't speak, unsure I could trust myself not to snap this point in time. After the hours of talking, yelling, and paperwork, I felt like a shaken-up bottle of pop with the lid on—about to go off.

"What happened?" Michael asked, his brow furrowed in concern.

I just shook my head and grunted, keeping communications to a minimum until I calmed down. "Need a shower." I felt frozen but overheated at the same time, which made no sense. But I felt contaminated and needed to wash the stink of those disgusting excuses for men off my body, so I marched straight to the bathroom downstairs so that I wouldn't wake our mate and turned the water on for a *long, hot* shower.

I half considered giving myself an orgasm to help with the frustration bubbling away deep inside me, but after a moment or two of stroking my own cock, nothing happened. If anything, the numbness only inflamed my anger. Agitated as I was, I forced myself to just stand under the hot water and will my tight, bunched muscles to relax. I felt like an over-tightened guitar string. I needed to get some slack back.

There was a knock at the door, and before I could answer, both Michael and David walked into the room. I shut my eyes and sighed.

Yep. No such thing as privacy in this family.

"What happened?" David demanded, leaning against the double bowl sink.

"Did you arrest them?" Michael pushed further, crossing his arms over his chest.

I sighed again and turned off the water. Clearly, that I wasn't going to get any sleep until the pack were satisfied. "We arrested them and booked them. They'll see the judge first thing in the morning, and he'll decide if there's enough evidence to have a trial."

Michael nodded and David almost smiled. "Good," they said in unison.

I grabbed a towel and quickly dried myself before wrapping the towel around my waist. "Look, I'm starving, exhausted, and need to see our mate. Can I fill you in tomorrow morning? I'm sure Matilda will want to know all the details firsthand too."

David stood up again and headed for the door. "Yeah, that's fair. There's some food in the fridge if you're hungry," he said.

"Or there're some ready-made protein shakes," Michael offered, which was weird, because he never knew what food we had. It's not the sort of thing he normally paid attention to. "It just depends on how fast you want to get to bed."

I sighed for the third time inside of twenty minutes, feeling older and wearier than I wished. "A protein shake sounds perfect."

It's all that I've got the energy for.

Grabbing a chocolate-flavored shake from the fridge, I gulped it down in a few swallows, then headed for the stairs with the guys hard on my heels.

I checked my watch. It was after midnight now.

Fuck... No wonder I'm tired.

"How long has she been asleep?" I asked under my breath.

"About an hour," David whispered. "She wanted to stay up and wait for you, but she was just too exhausted, especially after the hospital visit."

I glanced at my packmates' faces, which were now stitched up, but still swollen and red. "Are you both okay?" My hands tightened into fists, the rage inside me still boiling madly. "You did a great job on those brothers. They got what they deserved." All four of them had to go to the E.R. after their clash with Toby, Michael, and David at the diner. We were still charging them with gross misconduct, given they were the aggressors in the situation.

"Yeah, we're fine," Michael said, speaking for them as he lifted his chin.

"Before I forget, I need you both to come into the station in the morning to give statements."

"No problem," David answered for them both.

I swallowed hard as the next question—the one that had been haunting me all night—rose to the forefront of my mind. "Is Matilda okay? The baby?"

David grinned, his face lighting up. "Yeah, they're fine. The doctor even did an ultrasound to check for a heartbeat to allay Tilly's fears, and we're all good."

A strange happiness emanated from them both now that I'd mentioned her pregnancy, but I just shrugged off the extra questions. They could wait till morning. I especially didn't love the fact that I missed Matilda's first ultrasound, but I had my hands full with her wretched family.

A necessary evil.

"Let's go," I said. Together we made our way up into the loft, and there was our mate, sleeping right in the middle of her nest like an angel, where she liked to be most. I groaned as I tossed the towel away before climbing onto the mattress beside her. I needed to feel her warmth, to know she was okay. She didn't wake up but curled into me like she always did. I opened my arms, and she rolled over and settled with her head on my chest, a relief-filled sigh escaping her lips as she continued to sleep.

My two battered packmates undressed and climbed into bed too, and finally, peace descended on our home and in our hearts. We'd survived. Our precious Matilda was alive and well. I could rest. Everything was okay. I closed my eyes as David and Michael settled into their places. Together, we all fell fast asleep.

I WOKE up to the feel of Matilda's soft lips on my neck. I blinked against the morning light and squeezed my arms tighter around our mate. I'd held her all night long and never once let her go. "Morning, beautiful."

"Where are they?" she asked, her voice stricken with panic. "Are they in jail?"

I forced my eyes fully open and pushed myself up so that I could sit and lean against the pillows. My baby girl needed serious comfort. "Hey, it's okay. You're safe. We're all here and we've got you."

She bit her lip but sat up too, grabbing hold of my hand to anchor herself. "What happened last night?" she asked, her voice still trembling.

I squeezed her hand and gave her a brief rundown of what had happened throughout the night, concluding with the good news. "Your fathers' hearing is today. I expect they'll get at least thirty days each and be required to pay a hefty fine too."

Her eyes went wide, then she wiped away the tear that betrayed her. "And my brothers?"

I glanced toward David. "I'm not sure… do you guys know?"

"They were getting patched up, then they were headed to jail to join their fathers. I don't think they'll be coming anywhere near us," David soothed.

But Matilda wasn't having it. She grabbed at me again with greater urgency, her gaze dropping from mine to her belly. "I'm not safe here anymore. They'll find me. They'll try to take me again!"

"No, they won't. They can't," I said as calmly as possible. "We'll increase the security at the house and take out a restraining order on them. Don't worry, sweetheart. We'll have plans on plans on plans to protect you." But I'd keep those to myself until I could discuss the matter further with David and Michael.

"Okay," she whispered, though she didn't look totally convinced.

Michael stretched his arms above his head and made a strange morning grunting noise before adding to the conversation and changing the tone of the moment completely. "Hey, Tilly, why don't you show Patrick the ultrasound from last night?"

Her face lit up, and she scrambled over the blankets in instant excitement. "Oh, yes!" She hopped off the bed and ran for the dresser drawers, where she grabbed what looked like a small piece of paper and brought it back to me.

I held out my hand and smiled at my beautiful mate. "I wish I'd been there to see everything," I said regretfully. "I'm sorry, baby."

She giggled as she climbed back into the warm bed beside me and held the ultrasound up for me to see. "Don't be," she said. "I wish you'd been there too. But I understand that the law doesn't rest, and that you were just doing your job."

I frowned at the image, taking it from her hands and turning it every which way. "I don't get it. What's all this?" The blurry picture was labeled with an *A* and a *B*. No matter how I looked at it, I couldn't make out an accurate shape of a baby. It was a visual mess of black and white.

She laughed again and pointed at the picture, her tone full of warmth and amusement as she enlightened me to what I was seeing. "That's Baby One and that's Baby Two."

I turned towards her, my eyes wide as my heart skipped a beat with joy. "Twins?" I asked.

She nodded and put her hands over her smiling, blushing cheeks. "Yep. We're going to have our hands full. There are definitely two buns in the oven. They checked multiple times, trust me," she emphasized.

I grabbed for her and gently pulled her onto my lap, holding her tightly. "That's wonderful news, baby girl. The very best!"

Michael and David cackled with laughter and began telling the story of how they'd found out last night and how shocked they'd all been. I listened and held Matilda close, more determined than ever to keep her safe.

"Now, we're really going to have to get organized," David said, ever the planner. "We have two of everything to get now, and we'll have to move out of the loft."

Matilda giggled, shook her head, and whispered to me, "He knows there's space up here for two cribs, right?"

I laughed and tugged her even closer, relishing in her scent and the bliss of her physical presence. If our girl wanted to live in the loft, that's where we'd be living. Our family was getting bigger *so* much faster than I'd ever anticipated. We were going to be twin dads!

I can hardly believe it.

Now, all I had to do was find a way to keep them all out of harm's way—permanently.

CHAPTER TWENTY-THREE
DAVID

I closed the pharmacy for the first time *ever* and asked my
staff to put up notes in the shop informing the public of a
family emergency with my sincerest apologies. They'd all know what
was going on soon enough. Nothing spreads faster in a small town
than gossip. Not that it bothered me, or any of us, for that matter. We
chose a quiet life because we loved the sense of community that came
with it and wanted to raise a family in its safety and peace one day.

And now we have that chance!

Marie was already on the phone interviewing possible new hires,
which was great. I wanted at least one new pharmacist working for
me from now on, though two would be even better. There were no
awards for Overachiever of the Year out here. I'd pushed and bent
over backwards… and for what?

What was I ever trying to prove by doing it all myself?

I had new priorities now, and that included our beautiful mate and
her babies.

Twins! I still can't believe it. What a blessing.

"Hey." Tilly smiled as she greeted me, then slid onto a stool at the
kitchen counter.

I placed her plate of fresh waffles topped with maple syrup, candied bacon, and caramelized bananas in front of her. Feeding my traumatized and pregnant beauty was high up on my priority list now. As the self-imposed chef of the house, it was up to me to make sure that she and our babies got all the nutrients they needed.

She picked up her fork and poked at a piece of gooey, sweet banana, then stabbed it through a portion of waffle, blending the flavors appreciatively as I'd hoped she would. "Did Patrick find out what happened with the judge?" she asked casually, though her demeanor suggested she felt anything but.

The town's sheriff had gone into the office to check on everyone and hadn't called yet. "I'm sorry. Not yet, sweetheart. But I was thinking..." I trailed off.

She raised her eyes in question. "David?" she prompted after a moment.

Finally, I gave voice to something I'd been thinking for weeks and hadn't been able to muster the courage up to say. "What do you think about going for a drive today?" I asked.

"A drive?" she repeated. "To where?"

"To... your hometown?" I ventured as I leaned against the counter.

She froze like a deer in headlights, her fork halfway to her mouth. "My..." She shook her head as if in denial. "I'm sorry, what? Why?"

"Well," I placed both hands on the counter, thinking aloud. "Lately, I've been wondering how we can re-unite you with your mother. My first thought was to call her, obviously, but being under your fathers' chokehold, she probably doesn't have the freedom of a phone, does she?"

Tilly shook her head and shoved the forkful of decadent waffles into her mouth. "Nope."

With caution, I measured my voice and controlled my tone, carefully bringing light to my plan. "Okay... well, with your dads and brothers stuck here for the moment, maybe we should go there and visit her?"

Tears welled in her beautiful blue eyes. "Oh my goodness. Really?"

I smiled gently at her, seeing how much her mother still meant to her over the last few years of survival and pack-bouncing. "Yeah..." I said. "And you never know. Maybe she'll want to come visit us for a while. We have the space and we can certainly use her wisdom and help with the babies on the way."

Tilly's mouth opened and closed over and over again. I didn't say anything because I could see her trying to process it all. And far too quickly, judging by the look of it. Her eyes were darting around, and she was nervously tapping her fork on the plate, though she hadn't noticed. Then she sat up even straighter and looked me dead in the eye. "Can we go now?" she asked.

I laughed, then saw her eyebrows drop low. "Wait, are you serious?"

She nodded. "Yes. And just so you know, the drive is a long one. It's about twelve hours."

I grabbed out my phone. "Would it be faster to fly?"

She bit her lower lip, teasing it between her teeth. "It might be, but I'm not sure it would be cheaper if we had to rent a car or anything once we got there."

I pulled up the airline app and talked quickly to her about which airport was closest to her mother, and how quickly we could get to her compared to driving the whole way. Amazingly, we could get on an early afternoon flight and would be at her mother's house by dinnertime.

"Are we really going?" Tilly asked, blinking and wiping at her eyes as emotional tears flowed down her cheeks.

I nodded. "Absolutely. I meant it. I'm going to call Michael and check if he's coming. Then we'll leave for the airport. So, go get changed and pack a few things, sweetheart, and we'll be out of here."

Tilly raced around the counter and stood on the tips of her toes, pressing a kiss to my cheek. "Thank you, David! Thank you so much!" She squealed and ran up the stairs to get ready.

I sighed.

Shit.

I'd really jumped in before double checking… anything really.

"What's up?" Michael asked, answering the phone and listening as I gave him the quick rundown. He sighed audibly. "I'm buried here, and now, hearing this? I want to make sure that none of the guys get out of the hospital early. I'll stay and play defense, keep the ground clear. You go and get her mother out of there."

"Will do," I said, hanging up. It was up to me.

All right then. Let's do this.

I tapped on my phone, booked our flights, and rented a truck at the airport. We were going to have to hurry, but we'd make it. I went to my bedroom and threw a change of clothes into a carry-on suitcase and put my warmest gear on.

"Are you ready?" Tilly called excitedly, panting as she ran into my room.

"Yes," I said, throwing a toothbrush in my shaving kit, packing it away, and zipping up my luggage. "Let's go, beautiful girl." She squealed again and it was the happiest, most excited noise I'd ever heard *anyone* make. The wind howled outside, and snow was on the way, according to my weather app. "I don't think your brothers are getting out of town today," I said with a grin, opening the car door for her.

"Are you sure?" she asked, hopping inside.

I hurried around to the driver's door and jumped in, brushing the snow off my coat. "Yeah. The storm that's coming will hit in about four hours, and we should be well and truly in the plane and on our way by then."

She clapped her hands and laughed and stamped her feet in the footwell. "Perfect!"

With a grin on my face, I pulled out of the driveway and took off, grateful that we only lived forty-five minutes from the local airport. We'd need to take a connecting flight, but it was still only going to take a few hours in total. Mercifully, with the storm approaching, the roads were mostly unoccupied, and we arrived at the airport in record time. Not wanting to waste any time, I took advantage of the valet parking and grabbed our things.

Tilly had never been on a plane before and she clung to me like a limpet to a rock, clinging to my hand as we moved through security and made our way toward the gate.

Before we boarded the plane, she stopped dead in her tracks. "What if my mom doesn't want to see me?" she asked, her eyes wide and searching.

I smiled at her in reassurance. "That's not going to happen, beautiful. But if it does, we'll just fly home, and you know… move on with our lives. And you won't have to think about it or wonder *What if?* anymore."

She frowned and scratched the back of her neck, a nervous reaction. "That's an awfully expensive day for you, potentially for nothing."

I smiled again and shook my head. "Sweetheart, it's not. I promise. And I know what it's like to worry about something like this. Your peace of mind is worth *so* much more to all of us than a few flights."

She grabbed me tighter, her whole body vibrating as the possibilities came roaring back past her fear and trepidation. "Are you sure?" she asked once more.

"Absolutely," I said, squeezing her back briefly.

She inhaled sharply, then nodded. "Okay!" she agreed. "Let's do it."

I took her hand and led her safely onto the plane. It felt so good to have her all to myself. It's not what I expected to happen, but it was definitely a beautiful coincidence. I loved our pack, we all did, but we were all red-blooded Alpha men, and we'd be lying if we denied that we still wanted and appreciated quality one-on-one time with our mate, at least some of the time.

Once we'd taken our seats, the pilot's announcement sounded for all to hear. "Hello, everyone. Well, you're the lucky passengers that made the last flight out today. The storm is rolling in, and we need to get moving."

A general cheer went up all around us, and Tilly cuddled into me, closing her eyes as we took off. We didn't talk much over the course of the two flights, as my beautiful girl went inward. And I knew why without having to ask. She was worried about what was going to happen when we reached her mother. And in truth, so was I. But that didn't stop me from enjoying the peace and luxury of a little travel time.

By the time we finally arrived and had picked up our rental truck, she was shivering with stress and anxiety. "Put her address into my maps sweetheart," I said, handing her my phone. "Then we can talk on the way."

I'd been in touch with Patrick and Michael throughout the day, and although Tilly's dads were still in jail awaiting their hearing, her brothers were not. They were hurt but had discharged themselves from the hospital and would be on their way soon. There was nothing Patrick could have done about that. On the plus side, though, we had a good ten-hour head start on them. Still, I didn't want to risk my mate's safety or her mom's.

Tilly set the phone back into the cradle and the driving instructions began speaking over the speakers. It was over an hour drive according to the app, but we'd get there with lots of time to spare, I was sure.

"Okay, let's go," I said, pulling out into traffic and heading toward Tilly's childhood home. "Tell me what's going on inside your head, sweetheart."

She pulled a small, fluffy blanket from her bag that smelled like our nest and wrapped herself up in it. She shrugged and pursed her lips, obviously mulling over a million possibilities and memories in her mind.

I turned the heat up inside the truck, although I was pretty sure the blanket was for scent and reassurance, not for warmth. "Come on, angel. You can talk to me. Tell me what you're thinking. I'm here to help."

She shivered again. "I don't know. I guess I'm just thinking about the night I left. She told me never to look back. Never to come back. And now..."

I smiled. "Baby, I don't think she meant it literally."

"What do you mean?" Tilly asked, adjusting her seatbelt.

"Well, maybe she meant don't come back until you're mated. Until you're strong and happy and can stand up to your brothers. Maybe she meant not to come back until it was safe."

She hummed to herself softly. "Maybe."

"Sweetheart, look. Worst-case scenario, she congratulates you on your pregnancy and finding three Alphas that love you, then tells you to leave."

She nodded, but her pain was as plain as day on her face. Her lips trembled and eyes teared up again. "Yeah, that's not so bad, I guess." But her words lacked any conviction. "It'd be hard to walk away. But just knowing she's okay and surviving would give me a little peace of mind, at least."

I let her finish, then offered her my most understanding and encouraging smile "But," I said, "in the best-case scenario, she packs her bags, jumps in the truck, comes home with us, and lives happily ever after as a beloved grandma to twins."

Tilly wiped at her eyes and her face as though she were clearing away tears, although I hadn't seen any fall. She gulped. "You're right… you're right. Either way, I could never go back with my fathers there. You saw them. They would never have let her see me. At least now I have the chance to say a proper goodbye."

I grunted as I relived the memory of the night at the diner. "Yeah, I saw them," I said as I touched my eye. It was still healing, but I'd been lucky. I only had bruised ribs and a black eye to show for myself from the fight. It could have been a lot worse, especially if Patrick hadn't arrived with the cavalry when he did. Returning my full attention to the road, I suppressed a shiver of my own.

"Thank you for doing this," Tilly said, her voice quiet and soft.

I glanced over quickly, not wanting to take my eyes off the road for too long. "Anything for you sweetheart. Always."

We drove the rest of the way to her childhood home, and as we passed through the town, Tilly would gasp and point and tell me stories from her youth. Like where her school was and where her omega friends lived.

"That's my driveway," she said finally, pointing to a gravel road, the ghost of uncertainty in her gaze as it flicked across the landscape.

"We're all good, baby. We've come this far." I turned off the maps app and let her guide me the rest of the way. We rolled down that gravel road for a mile or so before Tilly pointed to an old weatherboard house.

"There, that's it. That's my house," she said.

There were dirt bikes strewn across the lawn, as well as tiny children's scooters and bicycles too. "Do your brothers have kids?" I asked, my brow furrowing.

"Maybe," she whispered. "They didn't when I lived here, but that was five years ago."

Five years. Damn.

"A lot can change in five years," I said. "Hell, a lot can change in five minutes some days." I sent a quick text to the sheriff, letting Patrick know where we were and that we'd arrived safely. I looked at our beautiful, brave mate and reached over to give her hand a reassuring squeeze. "Are you ready?" I asked as I turned off the engine.

A strange creaking noise sounded, and we both looked up as the front door to the house opened. And there she was… an older, more tired version of Tilly.

"Mama," Tilly whispered. Unbuckling her seatbelt, she got out of the truck before I could even think of stopping her.

I watched with my heart in my throat and tears prickling at the corners of my eyes as our mate ran full tilt into the waiting arms of her mother.

CHAPTER TWENTY-FOUR
TILLY

Tears flowed freely as my mother's arms came around me and held me so tight I could barely breathe. She wasn't angry at me for coming and she wasn't upset. The look on her face when I'd run at her like a little girl from the truck was the look of someone who couldn't believe what she was seeing.

"My baby!" she cried, over and over again.

"Mama." It was all I could say as I soaked up the feeling of her embrace. I thought I'd never see her again, let alone feel her arms around me offering that same love and protection she always had. It felt like a million years had passed between us, and yet none at all. After a minute, I felt David's presence as he walked up behind me and pulled back just a little. "Can we come inside?" I asked softly, meeting her teary gaze.

"Oh, yes, yes! Of course. Please, come in!" Mama waved us in and locked the door behind us. The heavy deadbolt slid into place, making me shiver with the memory of hearing that sound on repeat like a broken record from my childhood.

David stood by, a silent and patient loving protector as I fell onto the couch, still clinging to my mother.

"Baby girl!" she whispered, cupping my face as she sat down beside me, her heart in her throat.

I couldn't take my eyes off her. She was just as beautiful as I remembered. But the bruise on her eye was new, as were the many, many worry lines etching her face.

Mom squeezed my hand. "Oh, I missed you, beautiful. And you look so good, my girl."

I wiped at the tears that refused to stop. "Thank you, Mama," I whispered, sniffling.

She reached for a tissue in the folds of her skirt where she stashed everything—in her hidden pockets. "Here you go, baby," she said.

I laughed as she handed it to me. "Thanks, Mama. I'm sorry... I'm just... I'm feeling very emotional and overwhelmed."

"And pregnant," David added with a soft smile. "Don't forget pregnant, beautiful."

Mom stared at me, her eyes wide as they searched mine. "You're pregnant?" she gasped.

I shrugged and half laughed at the same time. "Yep. With twins."

"Twins?" My mother's mouth dropped open, and she pulled me in for another fierce hug.

I leaned into her because I'd dreamed about this moment so many times since the day I left, and I wanted to tell her this one thing above all else. "I found them Mom. My true scent match..."

She pulled back and stared at me, her hand straying to rest over her heart. "You did it?"

I nodded. "Yeah, I did." I sniffled again and dabbed at my eyes. "It only took me five years, but I found my pack, Mama. Three Alphas, if you can believe it."

My mother smiled, and her eyes watered, though she didn't cry. She never did. "I can," she whispered, a trembling smile on her lips. "I *can* believe it." Then she turned toward David. "But what I want to know is, where are my men? How are you here, and they're not?"

David walked forward and finally sat on the chair opposite us. "You haven't spoken to them?" he queried.

She shook her head, sitting even straighter if that were possible.

She was even thinner than I remembered, but just as strong. She was a survivor, like me. "Did they do that?" she asked, tilting her chin toward David's still-healing face.

"Yes, ma'am." David's gaze slid to me before he turned back to her. "That's kind of why we're here. Your husbands—" he began.

"We're not married," she interjected. The correction was wholly unnecessary, but I felt the pain behind her words. They'd never committed. They'd just kept her and bred her.

"All right then…" David smiled and coughed to clear what I could only describe as a very tense silence. "Well, your mates are awaiting a hearing over attempted kidnapping, and your sons have left the hospital and are on their way home already, we think."

I grabbed my mama's hand as a fresh wave of panic hit me. I knew my brothers were on their way, but I hadn't thought about just how soon they'd potentially arrive.

Shit!

She began to chuckle and shake her head. "Those idiots. I told them to leave you be, but they just couldn't let you go. They think they own you like they think the same of me, darling."

I smiled at her though my stomach was twisted up in knots. "One of my mates is the town sheriff," I said. "He didn't take too kindly to my dads literally carrying me off against my will."

Mama snorted, then her hand shot up to cover her mouth so fast it shocked me. "Oh my God," she choked.

"You can laugh," I managed to say. "It obviously wasn't funny to me at the time, but I guess it kind of is now. It was all kind of insane." And if I thought about it properly, it was funny. My overbearing and controlling fathers had received the notice that I was to be mated, and instead of picking up the phone or asking any questions, they'd just jumped in their trucks and headed across the state to bring me home and pursue the match they'd chosen for me.

They hadn't known that one of my men was the sheriff, that I was pregnant, or that I'd found my true scent matches. And they sure as hell didn't know that my men were never letting me go without a fight.

My mother stood up suddenly and walked over to the pile of mail on the dinky little table by the front door. She came back with a half-ripped piece of paper. "Your fathers pitched a fit when this came, but I…" She swallowed. "I was *so* grateful. This told me you were alive, and you'd found some men who wanted you."

"We don't just want her," David announced, standing up to his full six feet of height. "We *need* her. She's everything to us. The only way those men were getting her were over all three of our dead bodies. We'll never stop protecting her."

Mama's lips lifted into a strangely hysterical grin, and then it dropped again just as quickly. It was almost as if the very weight of such a smile took too much energy to maintain. Now that she was standing, I could see just how thin she'd become. Her old dress and apron hung off her gaunt frame. "Well… they didn't count on that."

I stood up, feeling awkward being the only one still sitting. It was time to ask the hard-hitting questions we'd come all this way for. "Mama, are you happy here?"

She turned to stare at me, her eyebrows pulled into a deep and perplexed frown. "Happy?" It was an entirely foreign concept, it seemed. With her mating, happiness was obviously never a part of the equation.

"Yeah, happy. Are you happy living here, being mated to my fathers, waiting on them hand and foot for the better part of three decades?"

"More," she whispered, and this time the correction was embedded with true pain.

It's been too long…

"More," I agreed, then continued. "Well, if you're not happy here, would you come with me? Live with us? You could be happy with us, Mama."

"Leave?" she whispered, then glanced around as if the walls had microphones, which, knowing my fathers and brothers, they very well could.

I straightened my spine. "Yes. Please. Come with us. Get away from them once and for all. You don't have to stay if you don't want to."

Her shoulders slouched, and she sighed as if all hope had been lost. "Of course, I have to stay. I'm mated."

"I have a lawyer friend who can undo that mating with a simple form. I'll pay. You don't have to worry about a thing," David interjected.

She slumped into the armchair closest to her. "I… All I wanted was for you to be free to live your life. To have a better one than me."

I fell to my knees in front of her, clasping her hands in mine with vehement passion. "I do, Mama. I do. And it's all thanks to you. I'm free and happy. But I can't leave you here. Don't make me. Please, please come with us. Before it's too late."

My mother's eyes were dull and resigned to her fate as I spoke. I reached up and shook her a little, willing her to rise, to fight, to survive. "Mama, focus. *Please.* You must listen to me. Once my brothers come home, we won't be able to come get you again. This is our one chance. The only chance. Will you come with me? Will you be my mom forever and help me take care of my babies? Their story can be different than ours. We can rewrite the future right here and now."

"But I can't leave," she whispered. "They'll find me again. They'll hurt me."

"That's never going to happen again," David said, his voice strong in the fragile room. "We'll buy you a house in another state if we have to. Hell, we'll *all* move. I don't care. We'll do anything to keep you safe."

Mama frowned as she lifted her chin and stared up at my wonderful mate. "Why would you do that for me?" she asked.

He stepped forward and crouched down as well. "Because you're our family now, too. You're our mate's mother. Come with us. Please. Let us return the favor you did us all that night that you saved Tilly from the same fate."

"They beat me that day even though I told them I didn't know where you were. They broke my arm and my ribs. I had to go to the hospital," she said, her voice trembling at the memory.

Tears slipped down my cheeks, and I silently sobbed, dropping my head into my mother's lap.

God...

I knew they'd punish her for my leaving, but I hadn't known how badly.

David made a strangled noise and held out his hand. "Let's go," he said with conviction. "You aren't staying here."

My mama's hand started to move at a snail's pace towards David's outstretched hand—one painfully hesitant and hopeful inch at a time. My heart was banging in my chest like a runaway train, but I held my breath and waited. We couldn't just steal her away. She'd feel forever guilty about it. We had to let her make the choice, and she had to do it in her own time.

Finally... *finally*, like a miracle from above, her hand reached David's and he pulled her to a stand. "Is there anything you need from here?" he asked her. "Not clothes... we can buy whatever necessities you need. But I mean mementos. Irreplaceable things."

She looked around for a moment, the weight of the truth hitting her hard as she shook her head. "No. I have nothing." Her voice sounded so small that it broke my heart. She'd been hanging on by a thread it seemed, and we'd come just in the nick of time.

I got to my feet as David swung Mama up into his arms, cradling her as you would a child. "You're safe now," he said as we walked toward the front door. "No one is ever going to hurt you again."

I raced ahead to push the door open as David walked through. It was getting dark now, and there were eddies of snow dancing in the air. "Where are we going to go?" I asked. "There won't be any flights in this weather." I opened the back door for David to set Mama on the seat, then grabbed my blanket and draped it over her, noticing how quickly her teeth began to chatter.

"Let's drive to a hotel and stay the night in the city," he said. "Not here. We want to get away from anyone who might know your family."

"There's a few in the city," Mama said from the back, her teeth still chattering.

David hopped in and turned the car on, blasting us all with welcome heat. "Let's go find somewhere safe to sleep the night then. We can get on a plane tomorrow, or I might even buy a truck like this and drive us all back. Whatever it takes, we'll make it happen. Don't worry, sweetheart."

I couldn't help the burst of happiness that pulsed through me as we drove away. "Really? A truck?" I asked. "You?"

He laughed as we picked up speed, heading for the main road. "With twins on the way, I need a bigger car anyway, beautiful. And hey, maybe your mom would like my old Lexus to drive around town? I'm sure she'd appreciate a little more freedom and independence, don't you think?"

We both glanced at the backseat, but my mama was already sound asleep, curled up in the warmth and safety of our truck.

CHAPTER TWENTY-FIVE
DAVID

I drove to the most expensive hotel in the city, determined to make sure Tilly's brothers couldn't follow us. I'd put not just distance between us, but a significant financial barrier too. I paid for the penthouse for two nights so that we wouldn't have to rush to check out in the morning. Our pregnant mate needed rest and so did her long-abused mother from the looks of it.

It was only 10 pm, but it could have been 3 am for all I could tell. It was so dark, and the exhaustion wrapping around us felt like a physical burden. "All right. Let's go, family," I said, putting my arm around Tilly's mother. I wanted to offer her my physical support without denying her dignity.

"Looks like the elevator is that way." Tilly rushed, despite her exhausted state, to join me in supporting her mom inside.

A young bellhop raced around the desk to greet us, eager to please. "I'll escort you all up." Clearly, the establishment paid attention to the comings and goings of their penthouse clientele.

The four of us traveled in silence, and I imagined the bellhop's imagination was in overdrive the whole time. Tilly looked amazing as always, but I was still bruised and taped up over my stitches. Meanwhile, Tilly's mother looked like she was about to collapse from exhaustion. Not to mention the fact that she was wearing clothes that were almost see-through due to age.

The door opened with a musical *Ding!* and we stepped out. There were only two doors on the floor, and the bellhop opened one of them. He handed me the two cards a moment later with a bright smile. "Here you go, sir. If you need anything at all, please let us know. The front desk is manned all night. Enjoy your stay."

"Thanks," I said, sliding him a tip as he carried our bags into the hotel suite and set them on the floor. The place was huge, but the only thing I was concerned about was security. "Don't let *anyone* up to our room," I told the bellhop with special emphasis and a stern nod.

"No problem at all, sir. Goodnight." He bobbed his head politely and took his leave, heading back down the elevator and leaving us to our peace.

I slid the privacy deadlock into place and almost felt a tangible sigh of relief fill the room around us as we all relaxed. "Well," I said to the women, "I think we need to order some room service first and foremost. How's chicken noodle soup, club sandwiches and a dessert or three?"

Tilly beamed at me. "Sounds perfect, David."

I grinned back. "Okay then, I'll order then let's wash the road off. There are two bedrooms and two bathrooms, so Mrs....?" I trailed off.

Tilly's mother swallowed and brough her hand to her heart as if overwhelmed. "Please, just Sally is fine."

Offering her a warm smile, I nodded. "Then, Sally, you're welcome to choose whichever one you'd like."

She smiled in return and shrugged sheepishly. "I don't know what to do. I've never been anywhere like this before," she admitted.

I glanced toward Tilly. "Okay. The food shouldn't take long at this time of night, so how about you and your mother check out her room, and I'll move our bags."

Tilly took her mom's hand gently, guiding her away. "Come on, Mama. Let's explore!"

Poor Sally...

It seemed she was in a strange state of shock. They disappeared through a brightly lit doorway, and I let out another sigh of relief.

We've done it! Thank fuck.

Without a second thought, I called down for room service and sent a text off to both Michael and Patrick, informing them that we'd picked up the *package* and were safe in the city for the time being. I also let them know I'd provide further details and take calls in the morning. The guys responded with a good old-fashioned thumbs up but asked no questions. They knew this rescue had to be handled delicately.

I carried our bags to the bedroom Tilly hadn't chosen for her mother and set them on the table by the door. The bedroom was absolutely huge, and I couldn't wait to spend the whole night with my mate—alone—in lavish luxury. The bathroom was just as exquisite. It boasted a huge bathtub, a double vanity, and the largest shower I'd ever seen. I could definitely see myself fucking Tilly up against those tiles… if she was up for it.

Hearing a knock at the door and someone calling out "Room service", I moved through the main area to answer the door. The server wheeled a cart laden with covered dishes into the sitting area, then left after I tipped him.

"Hey, ladies, our food has arrived!"

Tilly and her mother quickly returned to the main room, and we all settled in to fuel our exhausted bodies. It was satisfying to see Sally finish a bowl of soup and half of one of the huge sandwiches. It was likely she hadn't been permitted to eat well, based on her frail frame. Once we'd finished, Tilly walked her mother back to her room.

My love didn't return for another half an hour, and when she did, her eyes were full of tears. I pulled her into my waiting arms, walked her into our room, and sat down on the bed with her, holding her tightly. "It's okay, sweetheart," I promised. "You're safe. Your mom is safe too."

She nodded and sobbed against my chest, her gorgeous figure heaving with emotion and the strain of the stress. "I know," she whispered. "And I can't believe it after all those years of being terrified about never seeing her again. But now, she's here and she's going to be okay."

"Yes, she is, beautiful," I said as I smiled to myself and held her for what felt like a deliciously long time.

Finally, when her tears dried, Tilly slid off my lap. Her face was flushed with emotion, but her lips were curved into a cheeky smile. "Bath time?" she prompted.

I laughed. "I didn't run it yet. I wasn't sure how long you'd be with your mom."

"Well, I better get it started." Tilly rushed into the bathroom and turned the water on. I trailed after her, watching as she put the plug into place then turned to me. "Won't take long," she declared with a grin. Then she began to undress.

I stood, simply watching the beauty unravel before me. "God, you're gorgeous," I murmured, mesmerized.

I must be the luckiest man on the fucking planet.

"Are you joining me... or?" she asked as she slipped first one leg, then the other into the spacious, white marble bath.

I didn't need to be asked twice. "Oh, hell yeah!" I said, stripping off the clothes I'd worn all day. I groaned with happiness as soon as I was free of all constraints and stepped into the tub. The water was soothingly warm, and as I slid into its embrace, pure happiness washed over me hearing Tilly's gleeful giggle.

"How are you feeling sweetheart?" I asked. The bath was almost like a mini indoor swimming pool. Even with my legs stretched out, I couldn't feel her.

"I feel amazing." She smiled and paddled over to me, sliding onto my lap before wrapping her legs around my waist.

I leaned back and let my hands settle on her waist. "Damn, you *do* feel amazing," I teased.

"Really?" she asked, arching her spine so that her breasts pressed against my chest, then she kissed my lips gently.

"Yes," I groaned. "Really." Despite her playful advances, I had no idea where she was emotionally. Was she stable enough to make love to me after the maelstrom of the day we'd endured? The last thing I wanted was to overwhelm her or seem like I was taking advantage of her during a crisis.

She kissed my cheek, then my ear, and then my neck. "Mmm," she moaned against my warm skin, her lips peppering me in sensual kisses.

I scoffed as my body reacted in a natural manner. "Are you sure you're up for this, beautiful? It's been a long, exhausting day. There's no pressure here."

She slid her pelvis even closer, rubbing her slit up against my rapidly hardening cock. "I know," she crooned, her voice husky. "But I want you. I *always* want you." I groaned as she lifted herself up and wrapped her arms around my neck, her tongue sliding into my mouth as she positioned her pussy directly over the head of my aching cock.

I captured her mouth in a kiss of my own and pulled her down by her hips simultaneously, inch by inch. My rock-solid cock forged a path inside her perfect pussy, and I reveled in her delicious heat as she slowly engulfed me.

"Oh, my God," Tilly moaned loudly, her chest rising and falling as I filled her slowly.

Without warning—or having done anything different than usual—my cock began to swell in a way it never had before. "Fuck," I hissed, swallowing hard at the exquisite levels of ecstasy building within me as a result.

Holy damn. I've never knotted anyone before...

My mate gasped as she rode me harder and faster. "Oh, wow," she moaned, rocking on me and sloshing the water over the sides of the bath. "Fuck," she whimpered in the sexiest voice I'd ever heard. "It's *so* thick."

The power of my orgasm grew inside my body, and as it finally responded the way it should, my desire to knot my mate over-whelmed me. My pack brothers had already knotted our mate...

And now, it's my turn.

I grabbed her hips and pulled her down *hard* over the thickening base of my cock. "Fuck, baby," I growled, not giving a damn about the wet mess we were making of the bathroom. "You fit me like a glove."

Tilly threw her head back and screamed out with pleasure, her glorious breasts bouncing against me as she continued to grind and writhe, seeking even more intensity. Seconds later, she began to come. She gasped and mewled, her pussy squeezing and pulsing around my shaft like a wild thing. "Fuck," she moaned, stretching the word until it broke from her lips and she jiggled silently, breathless, red-faced, with her eyes squeezed shut as she rode the waves of her release.

I buried my head in her neck and threw caution to the wind, letting go of all control. It was liberating in a way I'd never experienced before. Her name filled my soul and the room as my orgasm hit. Pleasure coursed through me, so hot, fast, and constant that my vision blurred, and I felt my balls tangibly tighten almost painfully. My knot rapidly grew to its fullest, locking us together for all time as my orgasm assaulted me, setting fire to my senses as my cock pulsed and my seed filled her.

Tilly sobbed as she wrapped her arms around my neck, holding me to her as she shivered and shook with the strength of her own orgasm. Finally, when she was spent, she collapsed against me and we stayed like that—knotted together—until the water cooled around us, and our heartbeats calmed to a state of rest. Then it was time to ease out of the water and tumble into the heavenly king-sized bed.

I was finally mated to my Tilly, and she was already growing our pack's babies inside her beautiful belly. There was only one last thing left to do, but I'd have to wait until we were home again to make it happen.

CHAPTER TWENTY-SIX
TILLY

With a grateful smile at my mate, I reached over from the front passenger seat to my mom. She was seated in the backseat of the truck David had just extended rental on, sleeping peacefully, her head resting against the window. A sigh of happiness and relief filled my heart at the sight, and I squeezed her knee just a little to wake her up. "Mama," I said softly, coaxing her awake. "Mama, we're almost home."

She woke slowly, blinking her eyes and unwinding from the cramped position she'd curled herself into against the door. "How far now?" she asked.

"About five minutes."

"Okay," she acknowledged, smiling and nodding as she wiped the sleep from her eyes.

She'd slept most of yesterday, but clearly still had plenty to catch up on. I was ever so thankful that David had the foresight to book two nights in that hotel. We slept, chatted, ordered room service, and talked mama through a panic attack. But other than that, she seemed as well as possible, given the extenuating circumstances.

Goodness knows how little rest she's gotten over the last five years.

I knew she'd barely sat still before that, but I'd been there to help lessen both the emotional and physical burdens created by my fathers and brothers. Another wave of guilt washed over me at the realization that by leaving, I'd made my mother's life infinitely harder.

"Hey," she whispered, squeezing my hand. "Everything is fine now, sweetheart."

"It is," David affirmed. "And we're almost home."

I glanced back toward the road. We'd been away for almost four days, and I was desperate to get back into my nest and see the rest of my pack. I missed them so much that when I dwelled on the thought, it took my breath away. I loved them, and in truth, life only felt right when we were all together. "Have you spoken to Patrick?" I asked David.

"Yes," he said, sliding his hand onto my thigh while keeping his eyes on the road. "And your dads are being dealt with by the Omega Association. They'll be shipped out of state in the next few days."

I exhaled slowly. We had no way of knowing how long the process would take, or if we'd remain safe once my fathers and brothers found out that Mama was gone, but I needed to focus on the win for now. Patrick had already promised that he'd take care of Mama's protection also, so hopefully everything went smoothly there, though I doubted it would.

"Here we are, Sally," David said, pulling into the driveway. "Home, sweet home."

"Home," I agreed. I couldn't help but smile at the familiar sight. The sun was setting beyond, and its beautiful shades of pink, orange, and yellow cast our home in an almost magical light.

"It's lovely," Mama whispered as she choked up.

"Just wait until you see inside!" I beamed at her. "It's *so* beautiful. And everyone in town is really nice. You're going to love living here, Mama." A moment later, the front door opened, and Patrick and Michael came out. Michael basically jogged toward the truck, a broad grin on his charming face, while Patrick swaggered over, always the cool and collected authoritarian of the family.

"Is that the rest of your pack?" Mama whispered, her tone one of awe.

"Yep!" And it was all I managed to say before my door was yanked open and Michael bodily picked me up and removed me from the truck. I flung my arms around his neck and hugged him tightly, my heart singing as his strength and scent enveloped me. "Oh, I'm so glad to be home." Michael hugged me to him and carried me in without a word.

Once we were inside the warmth of the house, he set me down, and I walked back to the front door and pursed my lips. His gesture had been incredibly romantic. What girl didn't love literally being swept off her feet? But I had to make sure my mother was okay. "I better go help my mom inside," I said. But my guys had it handled. They were already carrying luggage and ushering her gently toward the front door. "Come on in," I said, holding the front door wide open in welcome. "Are you hungry?"

Mama had barely eaten on the road, but as usual, she shook her head *no*. "We ate heaps on the road," she answered. "I won't need to eat for a week."

David gave me a look that bordered on horrified, but I just smiled. I understood she'd lived decades in a state of scarcity and survival and that the bounty of this comfort and safety was just shockingly new to her.

It's going to take her some time to adjust.

"All right, then," I said brightly. "Which bedroom are we putting Mama in? Mine?"

Patrick shut the front door, then locked it with two new deadbolts that hadn't been there before. "Actually, Michael and I moved things around while you were away and set up space for your mom in his old room. We never leave the loft these days anyway, so while we look for a new house large enough to accommodate our growing family, she's welcome to any room. Though, mine's bigger," he added with a wink that made me weak at the knees.

Cheeky, Daddy.

"Oh, I don't want to be a bother," my mother said. "Honestly, anywhere at all is fine by me. If you have a small study or—"

"Mama, no," I said, taking her hand, my gentle statement brooking no argument. "Come with me." I walked her to Michael's old room, assuming that it wouldn't be set up for her, and that I'd end up taking her to the room I'd been decorating for myself, but Michael's room was perfect. My men had come through for me yet again. The room featured a brand-new bed as well as new linens. It was clean and bright and had been styled with minimalist flair. And just like a rented hotel room, it was ready for her to move right in.

"Oh!" I exclaimed with delight, my heart swelling with love. "You guys did a great job in here. This is just perfect, isn't it, Mama?" I pulled her into the room, pointing to the adjoining bathroom, which had also been cleaned and refreshed for a woman's stay. "And the shower in that bathroom is to die for," I added.

Michael walked into the room after us and spoke quietly, "We added locks to the bedroom door and the bathroom door, just so you feel more secure, Sally."

My mother brushed the hair from out of her eyes and stared up at my tall, gorgeous mate. "Thank you," she said, wringing her hands together, "but this is too much."

Michael chuckled with warmth and soft humor. "Hardly," he told her. "Just wait until we find a new house that has its very own fully kitted out mother-in-law suite."

Her jaw dropped, and I had to stifle the giggle that rose up inside me. She had never been spoiled in her whole life, but that was all about to change. An unexpected yawn caught me off guard, and I stifled it with my hand apologetically. "Sorry, Mama. I'm still a bit jetlagged, I think."

"Oh, you must be exhausted," she said, the stress clear in her voice. "Especially with the babies using up so much of your energy. Please, go rest. I'll be fine."

"Before we go," Michael said, gesturing to the corner of the room. "You're welcome to anything in our kitchen obviously, but we also moved a small fridge in here, just in case you wanted something closer or you have medication that needs refrigeration. We've already stocked it with food and drinks for you, but we had to guess at what you liked."

Tears slid down Mama's cheeks. "This is too much," she said again, her hand pressed to her cheeks in wonder as her gaze drank in the room.

"Oh, it's really nothing," Michael said, looking a little bashful.

It must have been his idea.

"We'll let you get some rest, now," he said. "We'll see you in the morning."

"But if there's anything you need," interjected Patrick, "we're nearby. You're safe here."

"Yes, of course. Thank you."

I rushed over for one final hug. "He's right," I said, pulling her into my embrace. "We're safe here. We'll figure everything else out as we go." I kissed her on the cheek and held her at arm's length, reassuring her as best I could. "I love you. Goodnight, Mama."

With that, we left her standing in the middle of her room, still clearly in awe of her new and luxurious surroundings. Hopefully, she'd have the courage to explore and enjoy a nice long shower before she could sleep soundly all night again.

Patrick was waiting for me outside the bedroom door. "It's good to have you home, baby girl," he drawled sexily.

I launched myself at him, wrapping my arms around my Daddy as I heaved a final sigh of relief. "It's *so* good to be back," I said, burying my face in the crook of his neck. His scent washed over me, warm, familiar, and mouth-watering.

He swept me up in his arms like a cowboy from an old western and started walking toward the stairs. "Are you hungry?" he asked.

I shook my head and cupped his beloved face. "No, thank you," I said, voicing my appreciation. "We ate on the road."

A wolfish grin swept his lips, the mischievous sparkle in his gaze giving me butterflies. "Then we can take you straight to bed," he said.

I snuggled into his chest and was carried up the stairs, then set on my feet to climb up the ladder into the loft. We definitely needed a better way to get up there, but tonight—as it had every other night before—it would have to do.

Maybe in the next house I'll make sure to set up my nest on the main floor instead.

I couldn't truly imagine leaving, but if the guys wanted something different, bigger, or more secure, I wasn't going to complain. Whatever they thought was best for our family was fine by me. I trusted them with all my heart. David followed us up into the loft and I turned toward him. "Where's Michael?"

"Locking up," he answered simply.

I frowned. What sort of security measures had been added since I'd last been home?

Patrick settled me into my nest and pulled the blankets up over me. "Don't worry, baby girl. We'll go through everything tomorrow morning. We just want you to rest tonight."

"Okay," I agreed, staring up at him, my heart full. He looked tired and there were dark circles under his eyes. "You look like you need some rest too," I said. I imagined they hadn't slept much while I was away. I'd had the comfort of David, but my other two boys had faced our empty house alone.

Patrick smiled, shrugging out of his shirt. "Yeah," he agreed. "It turns out that I don't sleep so good without you anymore."

Michael stood up from the ladder into the loft, smiling his head off. "Hey," he said.

"What's up?" I asked him as the three men all glanced at one another in turn, some secret understanding passing between them. "Uh-oh. What are you all up to now?" I asked. I was joking of course, but when all three came to sit on the nest with me, I wasn't convinced they'd understood. They weren't completely undressed or ready for bed yet, and I wasn't either.

Wait a minute...

Something seemed off or out of place, and worry hit me hard. "Do you need to tell me something about my fathers?"

Or my brothers, for that matter.

My whole male family line had been the bane of my existence this week. I wouldn't be surprised to learn they'd knocked out officers or had attempted to escape already. They really were just vile and uncouth, and I was glad to be free of them.

"No… well, yes, actually. But we can talk about that in the morning," Patrick revealed. "This is something different."

I sat up straighter in my nest and held the covers to my chest. They all looked so serious, and I couldn't help but worry about what was going on. "What is it?" I pressed, my voice trembling ever so slightly. "What's going on?"

Michael took something out of his pocket and handed it to Patrick. It looked to be a small box of some sort. Then Patrick popped it open and handed it to me casually. Inside was the most beautiful set of rings I'd ever seen—three to be exact. A stunningly large princess-cut diamond sparkled in a square setting in the center, the focal piece, nestled in on either side by two diamond encrusted rings. It was extravagant and classic and impossibly beautiful all at once.

Oh God…

"We weren't sure what style you'd like, so the jeweler said that if you wanted to exchange it for something else, we could do that," Patrick offered.

Tears welled in my eyes now, hot and fast. "What is this?" I whispered, holding the treasure in my hands like a precious star fallen from the night sky.

My men smiled back at me before Patrick spoke again. "We want you to marry us," he said. "Soon, preferably. Tomorrow, if you will. We want you to be our wife, our mate, and the mother of our children."

Michael nodded, his eyes bright and full of his trademark charismatic charm. "It's true, we do. Be ours forever, beautiful girl."

David grinned as he slid up next to me and threw an arm around my shoulders to squeeze me tightly to his side. "We love you, so much, Tilly. We'll do anything for you. *Anything*," he stressed. "But please say yes. Say you'll be our wife too."

I gulped, my throat thick with emotion as my eyes shed their burden, hot tears spilling down my cheeks. "Of course, I will."

This is a dream come true…

David cupped my face and pulled me forward for a kiss. Then he took the rings from the box. "Want to see how they look together?" he asked.

I wiped the tears from my cheeks and held out my left hand, hiccupping back a little laugh of raw joy. "Sure."

David slid the first ring onto my finger and gave the other two to my other men. I stared down at the first thick band of white gold and diamonds. "That's so beautiful." Patrick moved closer, sliding the second ring on to join the first. It was the classic centerpiece, the huge princess-cut diamond that drew the eye. Then, lastly, Michael slid the final band on, identical to David's, which completed the set. I stared down at the rings on my finger, never having gazed at anything so perfect in my whole life. "This is just… it's too much," I breathed, echoing my mother's words.

"Never," David said. "You deserve the whole world."

I looked up at his gorgeous face, still healing from his run-in with my brothers, and my heart skipped a beat. "I *have* the whole world," I answered. "I have you all, my babies growing safely, and now my mama is here with me too. I already have more than I ever dreamed possible."

My men crowded around me and took turns kissing me before we fell into a spirited discussion about the wedding and where we'd be going on our honeymoon. "I can't believe the waking world is finally better than my dreams," I said as the adrenaline of the past few days finally wore off. Wrapped up in the loving arms of my pack, we cuddled and I soon fell asleep, safe in knowledge that the men who would soon be my husbands—and the fathers of my children—were the very best men

in the entire world.

EPILOGUE

TILLY

Twelve months later...

I could hardly believe it. The twins were already six months old and the lights of our lives. They were rolling over, crawling, and generally getting into *double* the trouble. "Hey, Mama," I called into the kitchen where my mom was making fresh bread and Patrick's favorite ginger cookies. "I'm heading to the diner for lunch. Do you want to come?"

My mother walked out looking ten years younger than she had just a year ago. Her cheeks were flushed with heat and happiness, and her eyes were bright and full of life. She'd put on about ten pounds over the past twelve months,

Thank goodness.

She'd been frail when we rescued her and was still technically a touch underweight according to the doctor, but he was happy with her progress overall, and we were taking the best care of her.

"The diner?" she asked, brushing her hair back with a flour-covered hand. "But I'm cooking."

I laughed, my heart practically glowing in my chest. "Yeah, I know. But to be fair, you're *always* cooking," I said. "Anyway, I just promised

Hollie I'd bring the twins by today and I could really use a hand with them if I'm being honest."

Her expression immediately changed. No matter what she was doing, she always had time for the twins. She was an amazing grandmother, and I was more grateful to her for her time, labor, and love than I could ever say. "Give me five minutes to change and wrap up the cookie dough, and I'll be right with you." She took care of her baking supplies and then raced off toward her mother-in-law suite at the other end of the house.

About six months ago, Patrick had found the most perfect property for us. It was just a few miles out of town, came with excellent fencing and ample security to keep our family safe. It boasted a luxurious resort-style pool, six large bedrooms, and a completely self-contained suite just for my mama. We'd moved in just before the twins were born. They'd surprised the hell out of us by arriving a few days early, at home, with nobody around but my mother and my three mates present. That certainly wasn't the plan, but our girls had obviously been in a hurry to meet everyone. After a short stay at the hospital, we were all given a clean bill of health and allowed to recover in the safety of our home.

It seemed like just yesterday we'd brought them home, but the twins' growth said otherwise. Together, they played on their mats in the massive living room, happy and content as can be, while my three men were at work. It was a rare occurrence that they were all out at once. As a general rule, there was always one man home for protection.

"Let's go, beautiful girls!" I announced, scooping Lily up first. She was the spitting image of David, with her beautiful blue eyes and light blonde hair, whereas Jasmine had more of Patrick's and Michael's coloring. She was much darker, with oak-brown eyes and luscious chestnut hair.

The twin stroller was by the door, so by the time I'd loaded them up and packed a diaper bag, Mom was ready to go. She rushed to the front door and held it open for me. "Girls' day out!" she beamed.

I laughed at her gleeful expression, a sense of peace and warm fuzziness filling me to overflowing. After a lifetime of raising four sons—and me—Mama was in her element with two granddaughters. As we walked outside and into the sunshine, I sighed heavily, a wave of nostalgia and gratitude washing over me. "Can you believe this is our life, Mama?" I asked.

She smiled as we walked over to our new car, then opened the door to help me put my gorgeous, healthy baby girls into their new car seats. While she did a final check over buckles, I folded up the stroller. All of the twins' baby needs had been generously bought for me by my three doting husbands, who'd sealed the deal and married me before even a week had passed after their proposal last year.

Mama didn't really answer, but I could see the recognition and the appreciation in her eyes every time she drove around in her new Lexus, entertained guests in our huge new house, or cooked an enormous, no-holds-barred feast for my men. Like me, they lavished her with praise and affection for everything she did for us, every day. None of us took her presence for granted, and she was blooming like a beautiful rose in front of our very eyes as a result. She was finally able to thrive in good soil, surrounded by love and sunshine.

Everything about our new life highlighted luxury and ease because we'd collectively been through enough. We all deserved our fairytale *Happily Ever After* as far as we were concerned.

I hopped into the driver's seat and locked everything inside the house with my master key button. The house, the garage, and the car all rolled into one convenient little button. It filled me with relief to have. My men had invested in the best security around, so Mama and I always felt safe and never had to run around checking every window and door. Plus, the sheriff's office would be alerted immediately if any of the alarms were triggered at our home.

The drive into town was only five minutes, and the diner was just a few minutes further than that. By the time we arrived, the twins were starting to grumble a little for their lunch. "It's okay, girls," I told them in a soothing tone. "Grandma and I will feed you as soon as we're all settled inside."

I was breastfeeding both girls still, but had started them on solids too, taking some of the burden off me, which meant that the rest of the family could easily help out with mealtimes as well. Not that it was a burden to feed my babies, but with twins, it was definitely *a lot* more time consuming to sit around nursing both than I'd first anticipated.

My sister-in-law, Hollie, was at the door of the diner, opening it wide before we even got close. Her face was lit up, and she squealed with delight. "My nieces are here!"

I rolled my eyes at her playful way of ignoring Mama and me in favor of the babies. "Hi, Aunt Hollie," I said with a grin and a shake of my head.

Hollie poked her tongue out at me, then grinned and took the stroller from me. She wheeled the babies to our favorite booth, which was already set up with two highchairs.

Mama shook her head too as we slid into the booth. "You're all so well taken care of here," she remarked.

"Oh, yeah," I agreed. "Even though the guys trashed the place the day they fought my brothers, the owner forgave us."

Especially when the owner was part of the fight.

Mama nodded but didn't say anything. She missed my brothers, I knew that much. Even though they'd treated her as little more than a slave, Mama's trauma bond to her old life was quite strong. "Speaking of my old life... Your fathers tried contacting me again through an old friend. She didn't tell them where I was, but she passed on their messages."

I sighed. Those four assholes needed to just let her go. She'd officially severed the mating six months ago and received a nice settlement as well. Not that she needed it, but she liked having a little of her own money and independence for the first time in her life. "What did they say?" I asked, picking up the menus.

She smiled. "Nothing I haven't heard before," she admitted. Which meant they probably vacillated between begging her to come back and abusing her for daring to leave them in the first place. "It's funny..." she continued, running her nail over the table, tracing a pattern in the wood absently. "I always thought they'd move on quickly after me. They always said they would. They made threats over the years."

"What do you mean?" I asked, sliding her a menu before taking out the girls mashed avocado and pumpkin I'd prepared at home.

Mama frowned. "I mean… they're handsome and all four of them are Alphas. I thought… and they said…" Her lips pursed and her brows drew down in thought as she trailed off.

I couldn't help but laugh a little. "What, Mama? You thought they'd be able to lure some new omega into their home to be a slave for the rest of their days? All eight of them are still living there. It's a package deal, and who the hell would want that?" I asked. "I know I wouldn't want to take on the care of eight man-children!"

She sighed and smiled as she glanced up to meet my gaze. "Well, when you put it like that…"

I reached out and squeezed her hand. Thanks to her doctor's advice, Mama had been seeing a therapist for six months so far, and she was doing much better. But sometimes she had to be reminded to reframe some of the things from her past. Namely, that she wasn't the party missing out. She was free, she was liberated, and she would never be shackled to anyone against her will ever again.

"Mama, you were the best wife they could ever have hoped for. They'll *never* be able to replace you because you spoiled them for over thirty years, and no one else ever will. And that's not a bad thing…"

How did I explain to her that my fathers would never appreciate what they had? They were only mad that they'd lost it. But they still wouldn't ever be grateful to her for all the years she had put in. They believed they were entitled to her time and love. They were old-fashioned and set in their ways. Instead of viewing omegas as priceless members of society, they viewed them as the lowest of the lows.

"It *is* a bad thing," she whispered across the table. "I gave them *everything*," she stressed, "and they still don't understand that they treated me poorly."

I grinned at her. "Mama, I'm so proud of you."

She blinked at me and picked up a spoon to feed Lily. "For what?" she asked.

I took Jasmine into my arms and lifted my top to settle her onto my breast. Once she was happily latched, covered, and drinking, I continued, "For being able to see it now. You never deserved to be used and abused by my fathers, and I hope they're all starving and living in a pigsty of a house, waiting miserably for their fairy godmother to arrive."

Mom's laughter came out more like a scoff crossed with a hiccup, and she quickly covered her mouth with her hand, her eyes sparkling with embarrassment. "Sorry," she apologized. She never liked to make a scene, but it was honestly nothing.

I moved Jasmine from one breast to the other when she wouldn't settle. "Mama, the only important thing is that you're happy with us. If you are… you know you did the right thing. If you're not…" I let the words hang for emphasis.

Her eyes widened and she gasped aloud. "Oh, please don't make me go back. I'm happy! I promise."

As Jasmine plopped off my nipple, squashing up her beautiful face in sleep, I reached over the table for her hand. "Mama, you *never*, ever have to go back. Do you hear me?" I asked. She swallowed hard and nodded, her eyes filled with tears. Why would she ever think that was even an option? I just didn't want her to feel like she had no choice—my father's had done that to her for too long.

I only wanted to make sure that she was choosing to be with us because she wanted to; not just because we'd rescued her and she had no place else to go.

Without warning, David and Michael approached our table. "Oh, hey, guys," I said. "I didn't know you were coming in for lunch."

Michael dropped his head to kiss me. "Hollie said you were coming in." He smiled.

"What's wrong, Sally?" David asked, in tune with our emotions as always.

Mama didn't answer, so I filled them in briefly. "I was just telling her that she never has to go back to my fathers… unless she wants to, of course."

David's jaw dropped, then he glared at her. "Well, I'm sorry, Sally," he disagreed. "But I don't care if you want to go back. You can't."

"No way," Michael agreed. "We'd never survive without you. Especially now."

Her tears dried up, and she stared at me in question. "Why especially now?" she asked, her heart on her sleeve.

I giggled, still struggling with the knowledge myself. "Um… Mama… it's because I'm pregnant again," I revealed.

Her mouth dropped open, then she smiled, big and wide, and the light returned to her demeanor. "Oh! More grandchildren! My Matilda… I'm *so* happy for you all."

"Really?" I asked with a laugh. "You're ready for more crying, more diapers, and even more sleepless nights?" I wasn't sure my body was up for another pregnancy so soon, but it certainly thought it was.

"You're a blessing," Mama answered. "You *all* are. You saved me and gave me a true purpose. May your family grow and be filled with love always."

My heart sang with happiness. "I love you, Mama."

"I love you too," she said straight back, then looked at my men. "All of you."

"Then do you mind if we crash your girls day out and eat with you?" Michael asked with a cheeky grin.

Mama laughed and slid out of the booth so Michael could slide in. She wanted to stay at the end of the bench seat so that she could still reach for and feed the twins. "Anything for my sons-in-law."

I rolled my eyes at the favoritism and carefully handed a sleeping Jasmine to David. "You guys are incorrigible."

"What did I miss?" came another unexpected voice as Patrick appeared, tipping his hat like a true western gentleman.

"Patrick!" I grinned. "What are you doing here? We were just about to order."

He smirked and pulled up a spare chair to the end of the table. "I might be the sheriff," he said, "but I'm also just a hungry guy who couldn't wait to see his family."

With that, we laughed our way through a lovely, casual lunch and